HIGHLAND YULETIDE MAGIC
The Band of Cousins, Book 9

Copyright © 2019 by Keira Montclair

Printed in the USA.

Cover Design and Interior Format
© **KILLION**
GROUP INC.

HIGHLAND
YULETIDE MAGIC

9 THE BAND OF COUSINS

KEIRA
MONTCLAIR

CHAPTER ONE

PERHAPS DEATH WOULD BE A blessing.

In her heart, she knew that statement to be false, but the hunger had become a fearsome thing. Her own suffering was nothing compared to the pain of watching her dearest brother so close to starvation. Would they ever be safe again?

Shona MacKinnon leaned back against the cold stone of the cave, casting a quick glance at the others and praying she'd find more food on the morrow.

She ran her fingers through her brother Juel's hair, mussing it on purpose because it had always looked that way in the past, back when he was a careless lad who liked nothing better than to run and play outside.

Before.

Before the men from the Channel of Dubh had come for them, before they'd lost their smiles for good.

The Dubh men had killed their parents in front of them, set their hut on fire, and then dragged them away, slapping Juel any time he cried. The laddie was only five summers.

She'd fought hard, but there was little she could do against ten men.

But then the Lord had found a way to save them. Several of their kidnappers had left to attend to another group of stolen lasses, and one had returned in a right state. A group called the Band had attacked and killed his friends, releasing all of the other prisoners who'd been held in an abbey.

The man had other tales about flying falcons attacking his friends and Highlanders dressed all in black, but Shona focused on the fact that the other captives had gotten away. The news had given her hope and courage.

So did the agitation of their kidnappers. The remaining men were soon deep in their cups. Drunk as they were, they were careless, and one left his dagger on the floor near Shona. Later that eve, they stumbled off to meet with others in their group, leaving Shona and her brother tied up in the dilapidated hut with three other prisoners. Shona had seen her opportunity. She'd used the knife to free herself and the others.

Shona was the eldest, Juel was five summers, the other family consisted of two lads, James and Benneit, aged seven and eight, and a lass of five and ten, Jamesina, also named after their sire. The Dubh men had killed their mother, although their sire had been out hunting at the time of the attack. The children hoped he was still alive and would come searching for them.

Before leaving the hut, Shona and Jamesina had grabbed as many mantles and plaids as they could carry, knowing that it would be cold no matter where they ran. They hadn't dared to stop for over an hour to put on their mantles.

They'd attempted to find an empty cottage, but their surroundings had been totally unfamiliar to them. Not a single friendly face. At one point, Benneit had thought he recognized their surroundings, but one copse of trees was much like another, and they ended up going in circles. They hadn't gotten any closer to home, as far as they knew, nor had they found anyone to help them. Shona had decided they would do best to find a large cave in the wilderness, one to block the wind and the cold rains. It had taken her two days to find this cave.

When they'd located the cave, they'd only planned on staying for a day, but one day had turned into another. And another. Foraging for food was an exhausting venture, and Juel had become sick, forcing them to stay longer. Eventually, their collective weaknesses had kept them in the cave while Shona ventured out for food, and on the increasingly slender hope of finding someone to help them.

That had been over a moon ago, or so she'd guessed, the days blending together. They'd carefully divided up the woolen hose and coverings for their hands, putting furs underneath them to keep the cold of the stone from soaking in all their heat. If they hadn't, they'd never have survived the cold nights.

Here they'd slept, all huddled together, every night since then.

Shona spent her days searching for food. At first it had been easy. She'd found an apple tree and Juel had climbed up, dropping all the apples down to them, but they hadn't lasted long. She'd found some hazelnuts, but they hadn't lasted long either.

It took quite a bit of food to feed five people.

Shona felt responsible for the others. She was the eldest, at eight and ten, and the only one with enough strength left to search for food.

In her heart, she feared they'd all be dead within a sennight.

———◆———

Moray Allen sat in the solar of Muir Castle with Braden Grant, chieftain of this sept of Clan Grant. Braden's sire, Brodie Grant, brother of the renowned Alexander Grant, sat with them.

Moray had no idea why he'd been summoned, so he waited for his chieftain to explain.

"Moray," Braden said, holding his gaze, "the time has come to stamp out the remnants of the Channel of Dubh. The Ramsays and Grants are joining forces to defeat them. My cousin Roddy will be here on the morrow, and we'll travel to Edinburgh together. We could be gone for a fortnight or more. I plan to leave you in charge while I'm gone. Of course, my sire will be here to offer any advice, but I believe you are up to this task."

Moray sat up a little straighter, pleased to be given this assignment. There was no greater gesture of trust—Braden's wife, Cairstine, and her son, Steenie, would be staying behind. "Aye, Chief. I will handle everything in your absence. We'll continue our daily patrols and be on the alert for any reivers or men involved with the Channel."

Brodie Grant sat back, his arms crossed in front, his expression one of pride. Moray knew how pleased Brodie was to see his son take up arms against the Channel, the thieves and kidnappers who stole young lads and lassies and sold them across the waters. It would be a boon, indeed, if Braden and the others crushed the Channel for good.

"My sire and Corc will keep an eye on Steenie," Braden continued. "We know the lad tends to wander, but you needn't worry about him. You are to focus on keeping the castle free of marauders."

"Understood, Chief. I'll only take five guards out on patrol. The rest will stay behind to protect the castle."

Their clan was small, which made its protection more difficult. It was a challenge Moray had eagerly accepted when Braden had asked him if he wished to join the clan as his second-in-command. Together, they formed a group of twelve Grant guards.

"Chief, I am honored to be considered for such an important assignment. You can trust me to keep Muir Castle and everyone here safe."

Brodie Grant nodded. "Aye, all will be well. Go and put an end to this. Godspeed to you and all the Band."

Braden stood from behind his desk and clasped Moray's shoulder. "I have complete confidence in you, Moray. You'll do a fine job. We aim to be back before Yule. Cairstine is planning a celebration."

"I'm pleased to hear it," Moray said. "'Twas always one of our family's favorite holidays due to the fine decorating Mistress Maddie did in Grant Castle and the fine feasts she shared with the clan. The food was magnificent." Braden's mother had joined in the decorating. The dancing and the minstrels were a recent addition, something they'd all enjoyed. He didn't expect to see as large of a celebration here, of course, but a feast for all would be most welcome.

"Keep that in mind when you're out on patrol," Braden chided. "Bring down a fine deer and we'd all be grateful."

"Mayhap a boar or two," Moray said with a smile.

Braden and his sire began to converse on another matter, and since Moray had nothing to add, he said, "Chief, if you don't need me anymore, I'd like to take our men out on patrol. Mayhap take down that boar for you."

"Do whatever you must, Moray. Remember, if you have any further questions, I'll be here until the morrow."

Moray took his leave, waving to those in the hall as he passed through it on his way out to the lists. He trekked over the cobblestone courtyard of the beautiful Muir Castle and past the stables, stopping for a moment to speak with the stablemaster. "Saddle up five horses for a patrol, Corc. I'll be back with my chosen men in five minutes."

A wee face peeked out of a stall, eyes wide with excitement. "May I come along?" Steenie asked. "Paddy will protect me."

Cairstine's son, a wee lad of five summers, had charmed them all, and many of the inhabitants of Muir Castle were also partial to his pet—Paddy the Pony. Some said the wee horse was a magical being, for he'd led Steenie straight to Grant land after the lad had become lost in the dark. When Moray had asked Corc whether he believed it, the older man had swiftly replied, "Do not question why such things happen, lad. Scotland is the land of the braw and fierce, but 'tis also the land of faeries and things no Scot can explain. The lad was protected by our land and our God, 'tis all you need to know."

Ever since then, Moray had been a little uneasy around the wee horse.

"May I, Moray?" Steenie repeated his question, gazing up at him.

He hated to disappoint the lad, but he couldn't give him what he wanted. "Nay, 'tis too dangerous, lad. We're riding out to ensure there are no reivers or Dubh men lurking around."

At the mention of the Channel of Dubh, Steenie's eyes widened and he said, "Never mind. Paddy needs me here." The horse gave a whinny as if to agree with him.

"I'll see to him, lad," Corc said, motioning for Moray to take his leave. "Be on your way. You know he'll come up with another idea if you linger."

Moray left with a nod. He found his way to the lists, chose his men, and returned. They were outside of the gates in less than ten minutes.

"Which way, Chief?" asked one warrior.

Apparently, word had already gotten around that he would be in charge on the morrow. Moray didn't correct him, although he wished to—the position was only temporary, and he didn't feel he deserved the title that went with it.

"We'll head south. We have not been in that area of late."

They kept some distance between them as they rode, but stayed close enough to summon one another with a whistle. They hadn't gone far when Moray's eyes caught the glistening of something golden in the distance. Scanning the area dense with trees, he saw nothing out of the ordinary, yet he didn't doubt his gut. Something was out there. He scanned one more time, and then he found her.

A beautiful lass with hair the color of a beam of sunlight stood five horse-lengths away from him, staring at him.

Before he could call out to her, she bolted.

Unfortunately, he also heard the whistle of one of his

guards, followed by the clash of blades. He had to assist his men, but that didn't stop him from glancing over his shoulder as he approached the sound of chaos.

She was gone.

CHAPTER TWO

S HONA RAN AS FAST AS she could. The man who'd seen her wore a red plaid, and she wracked her starving, tired brain to recall which clan it represented.

Could he be a friend rather than a foe?

She hadn't lingered to find out. The sound of clashing swords had driven her away—and so had the handsome man's obvious interest in her. She'd raced across the glade, leaping across fallen branches and stones, until she finally made it back to the cave. Out of breath, she stood to the side listening, not wishing to go inside and upset the others by telling them she'd been seen or that there were men with swords nearby.

She reassured herself that they were safe here. A person approaching the cavern would think it empty—twenty steps into the dark interior, there was an abrupt bend to the left that led to the hidden section where the group of youngsters had taken shelter, concealed from a quickly scanning gaze. A hole in the ceiling at the back of the cave was just big enough to give them light without bringing in the elements of the outdoors. This kept them a distance from the blowing wind and eased the aching cold.

It would be a long time until spring, but they had to make do.

Her thoughts flitted back to that man and his plaid. Red. Hadn't her parents said the warriors from Clan Grant wore red? Everyone knew the Grants could be trusted, but they had to be quite far from Grant land. Her eyes had likely played a trick on her.

Once she was certain she hadn't been followed, she took the skin of water out of the pocket sewn into her skirts and went over to the burn to fill it with fresh water. It was so cold that they could hardly stand to bathe in it, although at least it hadn't iced over.

Failure pressed in on her. They were all starving, and this day had proven to be a total loss.

She sat on a log and sipped the water. What could she find them to eat?

Perhaps if she moved a little farther from the cave, she'd locate a castle. There'd be plenty of food to plunder from the kitchens. Most castles had stores of nuts, cheese, dried fruit and fresh baked bread, more than enough to share. The only problem was that Muir Castle was likely the closest, and her sire had warned them that a group of cruel men had overtaken that stronghold, killing most of the Muirs. The last thing they needed was to attract the attention of more bad men, but how was she to know which castle belonged to the Muirs? She'd never been there before.

Either way, they had to be close to some castle or homestead. The handsome man must have come from somewhere. If he'd survived the skirmish, he might be able to help them. Not all men were evil. The Band of Cousins had made it possible for them to escape their kidnappers.

That would be her next journey, but not until the morrow.

Moray trudged inside the gate walls, leading his horse to the stables. Corc was inside readying all the horses and saddlebags for the upcoming trip.

"Corc, have you a moment to answer a question?"

"Aye, Chief," Corc said with a grin.

"You need not address me so, but I think you know

that."

"Why not? You'll be acting chieftain on the morrow," Corc said, leading Moray's horse into an empty stall.

"Because it won't be for long," Moray said, watching as the stablemaster gave his horse a small supply of oats. "I'm sure the chieftain and the others will be returning for Yule. They'd not want to miss out on that. Once the forces of the Grants and Ramsays are united, they'll put a quick end to the Channel."

"I hope you're right. What was the question you had, Moray?" Corc closed the gate to the stall and turned around to give Moray his full attention.

"Do you know of a lass with yellow hair in this area? I saw her standing by herself in the forest."

"A lass alone in our forest? 'Tis mighty odd, I'd say," he said, scratching the whiskers on his chin. "Had she a plaid draped across her mount?"

"Nay. She was on foot wearing a dark mantle, and I didn't get a chance to speak with her. We caught a few reivers on our land, so I had to tend to that first. I couldn't leave my men to battle them alone. Once we sent them running in the opposite direction, I searched all over for her, but she was nowhere to be seen."

Corc scowled as he thought, rubbing his chin for a few moments before he shook his head. "Nay, not that I recall. But those bastards in the Channel had a sorry effect on all of us in the Highlands. People living in huts or groups of huts scattered for their own safety, though I know not where they could have gone. 'Tis a verra sad state, especially so soon before Yule."

Steenie came barreling out of one of the stalls, running so fast that he couldn't stop himself before he ran right into Moray. "Did I hear you say Yule? Is Yule coming? What do we do for Yule? We never did anything before. Someone told me once that Yule is for giving gifts. Or is it for getting gifts? Am I going to get some presents? Am I?"

"Slow down, Steenie," Corc said, his hands flat and facing the lad. "Sorry, Moray, but he is excitable about anything new that comes our way. Nay, lad. We haven't celebrated Yule at Muir Castle for many years, but your grandmama and grandpapa used to before you were born. I think you may be celebrating this year."

"If Papa returns in time," Steenie said with a pout.

"He will," Corc said with a reassuring nod, "and if he's late, they'll still have a celebration. Mayhap you could think of some gifts to make for your mama and your grand-mama." Corc leaned on the side of the stall, waiting for the lad to absorb all he was saying.

"And Papa and Grandpapa."

"Aye, them, too. We'll think about it. Mayhap you can whittle something or dry some flowers for your mama. You have time."

"I know," Steenie said, his face lighting up. "I'll ask Paddy what to make." He took off toward his pony's stall at the end of the building.

Moray scratched his neck in discomfort. "Does he really think Paddy will answer him?"

"Those two have a special relationship even I cannot understand," Corc said with a shrug. "He is the lad's only friend. It's a pity none of the guards who've joined us from Clan Grant have bairns. Steenie needs some friends. Friends who *really* talk. He loves the laddies in Loki's clan, but they're not here often."

Loki was Braden's elder brother, and although his family's visits were greatly enjoyed, they didn't come often enough from the wee laddie's perspective.

"True, but I think he'll be busy with his gifts for a while now."

"Lord above, I hope so. When he gets something in his head, he won't let go."

Moray left, waving to Corc. "If you think of anything else about the golden-haired lass, please advise me."

The look in her eyes, so desperate and sad, had made an impression on him. She needed help, he knew it. He would find out who she was if he had to chase her up one of the mountains.

CHAPTER THREE

SHONA TOOK A DEEP BREATH, trying to calm the rapid beating of her heart. If she didn't slow it down, she swore the reivers would hear her. But she couldn't leave empty-handed. She'd ventured farther away from their cave than usual. It had taken her nearly an hour to find anything useful, but her gaze had finally fallen on this small group of men.

They had food.

The men cackled about their feast.

"'Twas kind of you to let the woman live. The question is why?"

The man snorted, looking at his companion as if he were an idiot. "Because she had three loaves of bread, and 'tis entirely possible that she baked them. I allowed her to live," he said, taking another bite of the fresh loaf, "so she can make more. I've not had bread this good since my mama died."

The three men shared two loaves while the third one sat in a sack a distance away from the group.

That was the bag she had her eye on. They were drinking ale, and as soon as they were sotted, she'd steal that other bag from them. After all, they'd stolen it from an old woman, so it would be no sin for her to steal it for her starving family.

The skin of ale made its rounds, each of them taking a few hearty gulps. One of them staggered to standing, belched loudly, and said, "I hear something."

The other two jumped up. "I think someone's coming," the first one said. "Hush." He waved his hands at his two companions and they froze, standing directly behind him.

It wasn't her they'd heard because she hadn't moved in a quarter of an hour. But she did see her chance. The sack was less than a horse-length away and the men were on the opposite side of the clearing. If they'd just stay there…

She crept closer to the sack, holding her breath, when a war cry reached her ear. Three horses broke into the clearing, the men all wearing red plaids.

She reached for the sack and ran as fast as her legs would take her. One of the reivers yelled at her, lunging toward her with his sword extended—only to take a sword in the belly for his efforts.

She gasped, and then gasped again when she realized who'd saved her. The man from before. The handsome one who'd gazed at her from afar. "Halt," he yelled. "Stay where you are."

Shona ignored him and ran down a path that wove through the thickest part of the forest, where no horse could follow. This wasn't the first time she'd been desperate enough to steal from reivers. There weren't many of them in the area—she'd overheard one group describe it as a "wasteland"—but the ones who did pass by usually had something worth stealing.

When she finally made it back to the burn, she slowed her pace, stopping to listen for hoofbeats. The men in the red plaids must have stayed behind to take care of the reivers. She hoped they'd come out ahead. The number had been four against three.

Once she felt safe, she moved into the cave, sad to see the only one awake was Jamesina. The three lads were so hungry and weak they barely moved anymore, so there was little for them to do but sleep. She pulled the loaf out of the sack and held it up for Jamesina to see.

"Look. We were blessed today. Reivers stole it from an old woman, so I stole it back."

Jamesina broke into tears and whispered, "Thanks be to God. We will live another day."

Shona broke the loaf into two pieces, giving Jamesina the larger piece. "Here, you feed yourself and your brothers. I'll feed Juel."

She sat next to her brother and lifted his head to rest in her lap. "Here, Juel. I have bread."

His eyes fluttered open and he opened his mouth, much like a wee bird would do. She took a small piece from the inside of the loaf where the bread was softer and placed it in his mouth. "Chew, Juel. You must wake up and chew."

Her brother managed to chew, though somewhat slowly, and after a few more bites, he woke up long enough to say, "Your turn, Shona. You must have some, too."

"Nay, you need it more."

Jamesina said, "You must eat, Shona. None of us are strong enough to find more food. 'Tis important that you stay strong. Please eat."

Juel nodded. "Please, Shona? I'll not have another bite until you do,"

She hesitated, but then decided they were right. She bit into the loaf and almost moaned because it tasted so good.

This loaf was so large that maybe they'd live for two more days.

The only other thing she thought of was the intense gaze of the dark-haired Highlander in a red plaid garment. Who was he?

———◆———

Moray sent another reiver running off into the distance, his horse flailing because of the unsteady rider. They wouldn't be back, but Moray didn't like the fact that the men had been here in the first place.

What was attracting reivers this far into the Highlands?

While he knew he should give that question more thought, he didn't. Instead, he found his mind wandering back to the lovely blonde woman he'd seen again.

Who was she? And why did she keep appearing on Braden Grant's land? He still had no idea where she'd come from, but she could run faster than a deer. She'd had a package in her hand. Had she stolen something from the reivers? And if so, what was it?

He caught up with his three men. He'd left the others behind today, not expecting to run into reivers again so quickly. "Did any of you see the lass?"

Gilbert replied, "A lass? I did not see any lass."

"Nor did I," Clyde said.

Blane shook his head. "There's no lass out here."

"Aye, she had golden hair. She was on the far side of the clearing, carrying a sack, though I know not what 'twas. 'Tis the second time I've seen her." He scratched his head, unable to believe no one else had noticed such a lovely lass.

"Are you sure you weren't wishing to see a golden-haired lass, Chief? We've all been wishing for more lasses at our castle," Clyde said with a wink.

"I know what I saw. And 'twas the second time we've seen the reivers in two days. Why? What brings them this far into the Highlands in winter?" The lass's life was at risk with those reivers about. He'd have to patrol the area every day.

They arrived back at the castle just before the rain began. He made it to the stables so his horse didn't get drenched, sending his men in ahead of him. Fortunately, Cairstine's sire had believed in taking good care of his horses, so the stables were large and well-equipped, especially considering how few animals were kept there. Braden was always looking for more horses, oftentimes coming home with one whenever he traveled back to Grant land.

Corc moved to take his horse from him, but he waved him off. "I'll rub him down myself, Corc. He's a mighty

fine beast, and I wish to treat him well. Go for the others."
Corc nodded, and after Moray settled his horse in a stall,
he headed down toward the area where the food was kept.
Steenie was in the next stall working furiously next to
Paddy, who kept nudging him with his muzzle.

"I know, Paddy. I'm working as fast as I can." The boy had
his knife in his hand, and his tongue was pressed between
his lips as he worked diligently on his project.

"What did you decide to make for Yule, Steenie?"

He held up his project, which looked much like a stick at
the moment. "Swords. I'm whittling swords for everyone."

Moray nodded. "That'll be a mighty fine sword when
you finish it. What did you decide to make for your mama
and grandmama?

"Swords. I just told you." He was working again, his head
tilted toward the wood.

"Lad, didn't anyone tell you that lasses like softer things?
Like ribbons and soap."

"My mother's not a lass. She's my mama. And neither is
Grandmama."

Moray bit back laughter. It struck him that it would be
best not to question the lad's decision until he could offer
a good alternative. So what could he suggest the lad make
for his mother?

"Where'd you get that idea?" he asked.

"Paddy told me."

Moray glanced at the pony, who whinnied on cue while
tossing him a glare, as if urging him to mind his own busi-
ness. He narrowed his gaze at the animal, then chastised
himself for giving strange looks to an innocent beast.

He had something to work on—a gift for a lass.

CHAPTER FOUR

———

SHONA WASHED HER FACE AFTER eating another small piece of the bread. The sun had not yet come up, but Jamesina was awake.

"Jamesina, we must make a decision," she said, speaking in an undertone so as not to wake the lads.

"About what?" the other girl asked timidly. She was definitely more fearful than Shona, but she was determined, too. They were both intent on saving their brothers.

"We'll not survive here all winter. Not alone. There's not enough food, and our sources outside are meager at best. I know not where the reivers got this loaf."

"But what choices do we have? Those Dubh men could still be out there."

Shona got up and walked out to the mouth of the cave, waving for Jamesina to follow her. Once they were away from the sleeping lads, Shona turned her friend around and did her best to plait her hair. "Aye, they could. I think we have two choices. I've seen a group of men wearing red plaids who look as though they're on patrol. They appear to be protecting their land. They were the ones who sent those reivers running in the opposite direction."

"They could be the Dubh men."

Even from behind her, Shona could see how Jamesina kneaded her hands. Their worry would never end as long as they stayed in this cave. She had to convince her it was time for them to move. To take a chance. "I don't think so.

When they came to your home, do you remember what plaids they wore?"

Jamesina thought for a moment, then said, "They weren't wearing any. They had tunics and trews, with furs for warmth. What know you of red plaids?"

"The only clan I remember wearing red was Clan Grant, but we are a long way from Grant land, so it cannot be them."

"Mayhap they are related to the Grants."

"'Tis possible," Shona said as she tied off the plait. Turning Jamesina around to face her, she said, "One of our choices is to follow this group back to their castle or home, wherever they are from. I could ask them for food without telling them anything about the rest of you, at least to test them out at first."

Her friend gripped her hands so tightly, it pained her. "And if they're part of this Channel, they'll never let you go. We'll die for sure without your help. We just need to make it until spring. Then surely our papa will find us."

"You're certain he survived the Dubh men?" She had her doubts, but she didn't want to destroy the lass's only string of hope.

Everyone needed hope.

"Aye, he was not home. He was out hunting with five of our men. 'Tis why they came then. They killed Mama without even a question." She teared up but swiped at the tears on her face. "I want to find Papa. I know he's looking for us."

"'Tis true he could be looking for you. And he'll most likely go to the neighboring clans to find you. I could ask that group if they've seen the chief of the MacFees."

"Nay, he wouldn't. Clan Muir was overtaken by a cruel group of men long ago. Papa would never go there. There are other clans that are friendly, but how will we know for sure they're not from Clan Muir or the Channel? You must be careful. If those men you saw are from the Muir

Castle, they'll probably kill you." Tears misted in her eyes. "And reivers…"

They huddled together in the cold, waiting for the laddies to awaken.

"What was your other choice?" Jamesina asked after a while. "We cannot risk losing you. We'll all die. I know our sire will be searching for us. If we can stay alive for another moon, I'm sure he'll find us. There must be another choice, somewhere we could go to wait for him where we could be warm and safe."

"I saw a hut not far from here. 'Tis well hidden, and I think it would be plenty big enough for us. There could be food in there. It appears deserted, but I haven't gone inside yet. I've been too afraid, but each time I go out, I look for occupants or even tracks to the doors. I've not seen any. I think mayhap we could stay there until spring. I'm sure there must be pallets inside, probably a hearth where we could keep ourselves warm."

Jamesina's face brightened. "I dream of sitting by the fire at night, Mama telling us stories while Papa cleans his swords. If you're sure no one is there, then I say we should try it."

"All right. I'll check it two more times, then I'll sneak inside to see what they have. If naught else, I may find some furs and a wee bit of food." This would at least be a vast improvement over their present situation. She had to try it.

She moved back inside to Juel and kissed his cheek. "I'll go, Juel. You need a warm place. You've lost too much weight."

They all had.

She needed to change their situation. The danger didn't matter anymore.

———◆———

Moray wiped the sleep from his eyes the next morn. As

soon as he'd eaten his bowl of porridge with a wee bit of honey, he went into the kitchens to give his mother a kiss on the cheek. Making his way out to the stables, he reflected on how much their lives had changed for the better since coming to Muir Castle. His mother, Gelis, took a great deal of pride in preparing food, and she was a great cook. She and Hilda had built a wonderful friendship working together in the kitchens.

It took her mind off the loss of her two other sons.

It gave Moray a sense of purpose.

Moray's brother Ronan had been Braden Grant's closest friend, but he'd died going over a cliff not long ago. They'd all thought he'd taken his own life, but it was discovered that he'd been murdered by Keith, the third Allen brother, because of jealousy over a lass.

Moray and his mother still missed Ronan terribly. They missed Keith, too, although their memories of him were tarnished by what he'd become. Moving to Braden's castle had helped them to deal with their sorrow. Still, it was Moray's constant companion. He wondered why they'd died and he hadn't. He had difficulty sleeping, and often awoke gasping from a nightmare.

Until recently. Now, he found his thoughts filled with a golden-hair lass he didn't know. He'd dreamed of her last night, then he'd lain in bed for an hour trying to guess what she was about. He'd come up with nothing so he'd decided to check with a man with much more wisdom than he had.

"Good morn to you, Corc."

"And a fine morn to you, Chief," Corc said with a wide grin, because he knew how Moray felt about being addressed that way.

He wasn't the chief, just his second.

"I have a question for you. I saw that yellow-haired lass again when we encountered the last bunch of reivers. She was on the periphery of their camp, and I noticed her carrying something when she left. I cannot believe she's a wee thief, yet I can't come up with any other reason she would take something from reivers. Have you any ideas?" He leaned against a post, awaiting Corc's answer. He knew the area well because he'd live at Muir Castle for a long time. When the Lamont bastards had killed the Muirs, they'd spared the stablemaster. He'd stayed on out of loyalty to his former master—he'd felt it his duty to watch over Cairstine, his master's only daughter.

Corc thought for a moment, then said, "How big was the package?"

"'Twas a small sack. It didn't look heavy at all because she carried it with ease, almost as though it were empty."

Corc was mulling over this information when Steenie came running toward him from Paddy's stall.

"I know what she was carrying." He stopped directly in front of Moray and stared up at him expectantly.

Moray just quirked his brow at the lad, dubious of his claim.

"Paddy told me," the lad said simply. Steenie's solemn belief in his wee horse's mysterious powers always caught Moray off-guard.

"Now, lad, you know horses don't talk," Moray said, "so how could he tell you anything?"

"Aye, he does. He doesn't use words, but he puts the idea in my mind, then nudges me as if telling me to pay 'tention, just like Mama does."

"All right." He glanced at Corc and winked, out of Steenie's sight. "What was Paddy's suggestion?"

"She's hungry. She was carrying food. I think he's right. 'Tis the only thing reivers would have that a lass would want. They probably stole it first."

Having delivered his message, he spun on his heel and ran back to his horse.

Moray just stared at Corc for a moment, completely taken aback, then crossed his arms. "Hellfire if that does not make sense, Corc. What do you think?"

"I think I told you not to question that horse. I'm telling you there is a verra old soul in that beast. Do not cross him."

Moray wasn't ready to believe that theory yet, or possibly ever, so he returned to the idea that the lass was hungry.

"If I place a bag of food somewhere, she might pick it up and take it back to wherever she's living. Do you think 'twould work?"

Corc said, "Aye, if that's what her problem is. I can't think of anywhere the lass would be living. There's a group of huts where the MacKinnons and the MacFees live, but they are quite a distance away. She'd never come all the way here on foot, not from MacKinnon land in the winter. Other than that, there's only a deserted hut not far from here. Where would the lass be living?"

"I don't know, and that's what makes me so anxious. Tell three men we'll leave in an hour on patrol."

"Will do, Chief," Corc said with a nod. "And I'll have the horses saddled and ready."

Moray made his way down between the stalls to the one where Steenie kept his pony. It was the largest stall for the smallest animal, but somehow it seemed appropriate.

"Steenie, I've thought of something you could make for your mother and your grandmama for Yule."

"You did? What?" The lad jumped to his feet, dropping the dull knife he'd been using to whittle.

"You know your mother likes to decorate and this is her first Yule here with Braden. I think she would like some decorations."

"What are 'corations?"

"We could go looking for some pine cones and berries. A collection of them could be hung on the front door or gathered in a nice bowl your mama could put in the center of the table. Or we could fill a basket with them. Some holly would look verra nice, too."

Steenie's whole face lifted with his smile. "I think I heard Grandmama talking about 'corations. Can we go now?"

The lad didn't have a patient bone in his body, of that he was sure. Moray considered the timing and nodded. "Sure. I think there are plenty of pines not far from here. If you bring a sack, we can fill it and I'll help you arrange them later."

"Come on, Paddy. We have to go!"

The lad was fast on his feet, no doubt of that.

Once they were out of the stables, Moray helped Steenie mount then gained his own saddle. They hadn't ventured far beyond the gates when they came upon a row of pines. Moray pointed to a spot where they could stop. He helped Steenie down from Paddy and said, "There are lots of pine cones. We can fill your sack easily. Mayhap I'll make something for my mama, too. She has a new hut to decorate."

They filled the sack in no time and Moray was pleased to find a holly bush full of berries. "You may have to put these branches in water for a while so they don't die."

When they finished, Steenie hung his sack on Paddy's saddle. Paddy took one whiff of the bag and started to act up, swinging his head and stomping his hooves on the ground. He blew twice on Steenie and the boy became upset.

"Paddy, please don't be mad at me. What have I done wrong? These are for Mama and Moray's mama."

The horse moved over to Moray and nudged him. Hard.

"Your horse wants to knock me over!" he said, taking a step back.

The wee beast snorted two more times and shook his head again, as if to say it was frustrated with Moray, then moved over to Steenie's side.

"What is it you want?" the lad asked his pet.

Steenie stood very quietly while the pony rested his head on the lad's shoulder. "All right, but I've already made two."

Paddy used his hoof to paw the ground three times. "Three more swords? But why? Oh, all right. Three more."

Moray waited for the lad to explain himself, but instead, Steenie ran off toward the bushes. "What did he say, Steenie?"

"I must make more swords. At least three. I have to go find some more large branches."

Moray wasn't about to argue, so he followed the lad back into the trees and helped him find three stout branches big enough to whittle down. Then he led the ornery beast and Steenie back through the gates.

When they returned to the stables, Steenie took his findings and stored them carefully in the cupboard.

Corc pulled Moray aside. "I've made up a sack for you." He lifted the bulging bag up, then handed it to him. "I put a fresh loaf of bread, two apples, some carrots, and a few turnips inside. Don't let Steenie see the apples or the carrots. He'll want them for the horse. The wee beast wishes to eat better than we do."

Moray took the sack and peeked inside. "'Tis quite a bit of food, Corc."

Corc sighed. "I hate the thought of a young lass starving out there in the wild. If she finds the sack, see if you can tell where she's from. We'd welcome her here, no matter who is with her."

Moray nodded. They had plenty of room in this large castle. They'd started building a few more huts in the hopes that more people would join them over the winter. Braden had even discussed the possibility of bringing home some of the Channel of Dubh's victims.

Could this lass possibly have something to do with the Channel?

CHAPTER FIVE

S HONA EXPLORED THE ABANDONED HUT, pleased to see that nothing had been disturbed for a long time. There was no sign of anyone having entered either the front or back entrance, and they could easily sneak out the back if anyone did return to the cottage.

It was large enough for all of them, though there were only four pallets at the farthest end. Two large chairs sat in front of the hearth, and six stools surrounded the table in the middle of the chamber. There were utensils near the hearth, and a large pot hung over the fire as if it had been used recently, but there was nothing inside, not even any residue.

Pleased to see a good supply of wood in a basket next to the hearth, she checked outside and found a large stack piled behind the cottage. Whoever had lived here had planned on being in residence all winter. That thought gave her pause, although the former residents had clearly moved on. If she brought the others here, she'd be able to warm Juel by the fire every night.

Moving back inside, she searched through the cupboards, but found no food at all. Perhaps reivers had already cleaned out all the foodstuffs.

Rifling through the one chest between two pallets, she did find several furs and a night rail. She'd give it to James-ina.

She left the cottage, taking as many furs as she could

carry. Although the hut was a promising development, it wouldn't put food in their bellies. She still needed to find nourishment for the others. She did her usual foray through the woods, hoping something would appear out of nowhere, either a pile of nuts, some apples newly fallen from a tree, or a vine of beans or peas she'd missed before.

Nothing.

She sighed, telling herself not to be too discouraged because there was still enough bread for one more day.

But what would happen then?

Going back to the reivers' camp, she searched the area for anything she could take back. She was just about to leave when she noticed something that had not been there the previous day.

A large sack leaned against a tree.

Scanning the area for anyone at all, she crept over to see what was inside.

Her mouth watered as she looked inside: turnips, three carrots, two apples, and a fresh loaf of bread. It was a sack from an angel. She stood there holding the sack tightly to her chest, staring around the area again. Someone had put that bag there, but who?

And, more importantly, why?

If she took it, she'd be stealing. True, she'd stolen bread the other day, but the reivers had admitted they'd stolen it, so she hadn't felt it was wrong to take it for her family. But this…this would feed them for days.

This would keep them alive until Yule.

Tears flooded her cheeks at her good fortune. Trying to believe that the Lord had put it there because he'd known how much they needed it, she couldn't shake the knowledge that a person had put it there from Him. But that didn't stop her.

She had to take it.

It was a matter of life or death.

———◆———

Moray watched the lass struggle with the decision of what to do with the sack of food. *Take it!*

Either she wasn't as starving as he'd thought, or she had a high moral code that made stealing difficult for her.

How he wished to shout at her. *It's not stealing! Take it.*

After much thought, she hugged the sack to her chest and walked off in a direction opposite from Muir Castle.

He let her get ahead of him, not wanting to alert her to his presence just yet, and then followed her. They'd crept along like that for maybe half an hour when she suddenly stilled. He did the same, listening for any abnormal sounds. Her head turned around, but then she surprised him.

She broke into a dead run, the sack held tightly to her chest.

They ran and ran until he thought his lungs would burst in the cold. The lass was quick, that was for sure, quicker than he was because he couldn't catch her. He yelled to her, "Wait, I only wish to help you."

She ignored him, racing on as if he were a murderer. Then he saw the abandoned hut Corc had mentioned ahead of them. This had to be where she was hiding. Relief washed through him. He'd finally be able to stop running at that awful pace she'd maintained. Sure enough, she snuck inside the cottage as quietly as could be.

Then he was stuck. How to approach her?

For all he knew, someone else could be inside—her parents maybe. Not wishing to alarm anyone, he approached the door and politely knocked.

Nothing.

Dead silence.

He knocked again with the same result. He opened the door, peering into the musty interior. Dark. The hut was nestled in a cluster of tall pines and there were no tallows lit.

Empty. What the hell?

He opened the door and searched the cabin, yelling a few times—"Anyone there?"—but he found nothing to indicate she'd been there except her footprints. When he finally looked down, he followed the wetness from her boots over to a door.

A back door. The wee trickster had played him well.

He opened the door and peered out.

She'd be so far ahead of him, he'd have no chance of catching her now.

He held onto the door handle and yelled, "I'm not here to hurt you. I left the food for you."

———————

Shona went through the food sack with Jamesina, trying to divvy up the foodstuffs. She took the fresh loaf of bread out and said, "We'll start with this." She cut off two hunks of bread with a knife she kept in her mantle pocket and eyed the two apples.

Juel sat up and said, "Is that not an apple? I'd love a portion of that."

"Juel, because I'm so pleased to see you awake, we'll share the smaller one and give the larger one to the MacFees."

Jamesina said, "I think we'll eat ours today. We can save the turnips and carrots for another day."

They ate in silence, the chomping of the apples the loudest. Benneit and James were also awake, thrilled to see they had two different things to eat. "'Tis a Yuletide gift for certes," James said. "I wonder where it all came from."

Shona knew, but she bit her tongue. The lads didn't seem to notice, but Jamesina caught on quickly. "You know where this is from?" she asked quietly.

Shona sighed and set her apple core down, looking at her four companions. "I think the man in the red plaid left it for us. I found it back in the camp where the reivers were, and I know 'twasn't there before. He saw me and chased me."

Jamesina gasped audibly. "How did you get away? Did you lead him to us? Has he gone to find more men to come and steal us away?" She stood up, grabbing a few items and stuffing them into her pockets. "We must leave."

"Nay, do not worry. I led him to the hut and then ran out the back door. He never followed me so we're safe." She kept the words he'd yelled after her a secret. Although she thought there was a strong chance that he could be from a neighboring clan, she knew she'd never convince Jamesina to trust him. Somehow, she had to get the nerve to talk to him.

Jamesina nodded and sat back down. She took a small bite of bread and moaned. "This bread is absolutely delicious. Better than the other one. I'd like to meet the woman who made it. 'Tis heavenly."

Juel added, "And this apple is, too."

"But you know what this means, Shona," Jamesina said between bites of her food.

"That we might live until Yule?"

"Nay, although I do believe we will. This means we cannot move into that cottage. He's been there now. He'd know where to find us."

Which was exactly what she had feared Jamesina would think.

She never should have told her.

CHAPTER SIX

M ORAY CURSED HIMSELF FOR BEING such a
fool. The lass had bested him, without a doubt. He
mounted his horse and headed back to Muir Castle. Who
the hell was she? Why was she so desperate for food?

He feared he'd never know.

Once he entered the stables, Corc caught up with him
right away. "She took the bait, did she?"

"Aye, she did, but she used trickery and I lost her."

Corc chuckled. "Och, lad. 'Tis good to see you chal-
lenged by a lass. She's caught your fancy for sure. Is she old
enough for you to steal her away and marry her the way
they do in some areas?"

The twinkle in the old man's eyes told Moray that he
was teasing. "I would never do such a thing, but aye, she's
old enough. I just can't figure out where she's living or
why she has no food. It seems impossible that a lass that
young would be taking care of herself. And by the amount
of food I've seen her take, I'm thinking she's not alone."

"It cannot be a husband, or he'd be searching for food.
God strike the man dead who makes his wife do the hunting. She must be alone."

"Or with another lass?"

"I have no answer for you, laddie. Have you asked your
mother what she thinks? She and Hilda could probably
come up with a better idea than me."

Moray sighed because he had indeed asked his mother

for her thoughts the night before.

"Och," the older man said, clucking his tongue. "I hear my answer on that. It did not go well."

Moray tipped his head back and forth a couple of times then admitted, "She thinks I'm obsessed with my brothers. That I'm trying to atone for what happened to them by saving this lass."

Corc tipped his head and nodded slowly. "There could be some wisdom there, laddie. Think on it. Have you felt some guilt over your brothers? Because the tales I've heard indicate you had naught to do with their death."

"I did not." But he still felt guilty for being the only one still alive.

Why, he couldn't say, but he did.

A wee voice from behind him said, "He's not a laddie, Corc. I am. Moray is a man or a lad, but not a laddie."

"Och, laddie, 'tis what I call anyone who's much younger than I am. Corc is getting old now, you hear me? Be kind to your elders. Now, how are those gifts for Yule coming along?"

"Good. My grandmama is going to help me." With that, the lad scampered back into Paddy's stall.

A few moments later, Celestina Grant entered the stables. The years had been kind to the woman. Moray's tongue tended to tie itself into knots whenever she was near.

"Greetings, my lady," he said.

"Greetings, Moray. All is well on the patrol? Hilda thinks there's a storm brewing. What do you think?" She fluffed her skirts, giving them a shake, though he knew not why.

"Could be true. Clyde said he saw a halo around the sun this morn. And you know the squirrels have been extra busy during autumn."

"I'm here to help Steenie make a Yuletide gift for his mama. My thanks for helping him to gather the cones and berries."

"Surely was my pleasure, my lady." His hands fumbled

for something to do, so he reached for a length of rope, untying the knots someone had put in it. Anything to keep his mind off the woman in front of him. Her ethereal beauty unsettled him, almost as if she weren't quite an earthly being.

Celestina began to hum as she headed down the middle of the stables, stopping to pet a nose or two. By his guess, the horses were as fond of her as were the guards. They all seemed to lose their tongues whenever she was near.

"She is a bonny sight, is she not?" Corc whispered behind his back. "The horses love her the same way the Grant horses take to Maddie Grant. Those big stallions are like simpering bairns in a cradle around Alex's wife."

Moray couldn't help but admire the woman as she made her way past all the animals, not ignoring any of them, giving them each their due.

Corc chuckled behind him. "They're no different than your guards, Chief. They'd act the same if she'd bestow a smile on them."

Moray gave Corc a fierce scowl, indicating he wouldn't discuss such a thing around the lady.

Steenie came flying out of the back stall again, his eyes luminous. "Grandmama! Are you here to help me with my gift?"

"Aye, it is exactly why I'm here." Her voice had a unique rhythm—she'd been brought up by an Englishman, but she'd adapted many of the Scottish words and dialect.

Steenie gave her a fierce hug around the waist. "Grandmama, why are you so nice? You're nicer than anyone I knew before I met you."

"Why not be nice? It is much more pleasing to have people smile back at you, don't you think? Surely being kind to others will make your day better."

"I guess. Paddy, please be nice to Grandmama. She's to help us make Mama's gift." He hurried into the corner to grab the sack with the pine cones and other items they'd gathered. Holding it up to show her, his face let her know how proud he was of his collection. "See. Didn't Moray and I do a fine job?"

Celestina turned around and said, "Thank you again, Moray. Would you do me another favor and grab the basket my husband set on the top shelf in the cupboard? We'll be working with that one. And there's also a supply of ribbons up there."

Moray did as she asked while Corc returned to his tasks as stablemaster.

Once he brought the basket to her, she said, "Steenie, once we're done arranging the things you and Moray found into this basket, we can add a bow with these ribbons. It will look quite lovely on the table next to the hearth."

She found a small work table and moved it near their area. "We can do it right here. There are plenty of supplies for us to make hanging decorations, too, like Moray suggested."

Paddy began to make a ruckus. Moray headed toward the small horse and said, "There will be no causing trouble inside or I'll take you out. Calm your attitude, Paddy."

But the wee horse didn't seem inclined to take his advice. His tail swished back and forth rapidly, and his nostrils became tight and drawn.

"Steenie, I think you need to come out of there," Moray said with a frown. "I don't want you hurt by the beast."

"Paddy would never hurt me," Steenie declared, upset by the suggestion.

Moray didn't like the look of the horse. He'd spent enough time around horses to learn a thing or two about their body language.

Celestina strolled back over to Paddy. Petting his muzzle, she cooed soft words to him. The wee beast's attitude changed right away, but as soon as she was done, he moved over to Moray and began to push him with his muzzle.

"What the hell?" Moray asked—and then immediately apologized to Celestina for his language. The strange pony could be infuriating at times. Then Paddy walked over to Steenie and looked as if he were whispering into the lad's ear. When he finished, he returned to Moray, who stood with a gaping mouth, and pushed him again.

"What's going on with your pet, Steenie? Why is he pushing me?"

Steenie lifted his head for a moment as if he were listening to someone, then said, "Paddy said we can only make one basket, Grandmama, then we must use the ribbons to make pretty ties for hair."

Steenie looked surprised, then asked his horse, "But why? I wished to make more 'corations."

He listened quietly, then his shoulders slumped.

"Paddy says one basket for Mama, then hair ribbons. Two of them, and he's pushing Moray because you're supposed to be patrolling."

Moray couldn't help but laugh. "Now you're giving me orders, Paddy? Don't forget I'm the acting chief right now. I don't need the advice of a wee pony to do my job."

Moray used his natural swagger to exit the stable, shaking his head over the horse's antics. A rustling sound caught his ears, and he spun around just in time to hear the horse running.

Straight at him.

So he hurried out of the stable.

Paddy pushed against him again, more insistent this time. He only stopped when Brodie Grant emerged from the great hall and whistled at the beast.

"Paddy, go back inside. You'll not be bothering our chief with your problems. They can wait until Braden returns."

Paddy stopped in front of Brodie, gave him an aggravated snort, then returned to the stables.

"He listens to you?" Moray asked, surprised.

"He does. I'm not sure why. He listens to Braden, too,

but I think it's only because I told the animal he had to listen to his chief." He chuckled. "You cannot question he's an unusual creature. We need to distract Steenie. His mother is coming out to get a good look at Paddy."

Moray asked, "At the pony?" in disbelief. Had he heard him correctly?

"Aye, join me. We have to distract Steenie." Brodie headed into the stables, Moray directly behind him.

They hadn't gone far when a loud voice carried out of the stall at the back. "Grandpapa," Steenie shouted loud enough for anyone in the keep to hear him. "Why are you here?"

Without giving Brodie time to answer, he came scampering out of the stall, a huge grin on his face. "Grandmama was just helping me with Mama's Yule gift. Promise not to tell?"

"Aye, I promise, but you better hide it quickly. Your mother is on her way out here."

Steenie squealed and ran back to the place where he'd left the basket. Moray could hear him explaining the problem to his grandmama, and the basket was safely hidden away just before Cairstine strode inside. She gave a pointed look at Brodie, who said, "Steenie, here comes your mother. Please join us."

Steenie charged out of the work stall and said, "Greetings, Mama. You cannot go back there."

She grinned but played along with him. "I think Grandpapa needs your help."

She tipped her head toward Brodie, who quickly chimed in. "I wish to find two more branches to whittle. Will you not help me? You seem to have a special talent for it."

Steenie, seemingly thrilled by the request, said, "I'm coming, Grandpapa. We should go now before the storm comes along."

Brodie said, "I think we have time."

The two headed out of the stables, Corc winking at Brodie as they left. Moray sauntered down the passageway to Paddy's stall. The two women were back there with the temperamental beast, and he didn't expect the pony to be pleased about it.

Which was why he was so shocked by what he saw.

Celestina had some grain in her hand, and Paddy was busy trying to eat it, tipping his head every now and then to swallow. Cairstine, in the meantime, circled the small horse as if appraising him for something.

Moray asked, "What is she doing?"

Corc followed him and said, "Another Yuletide tradition. Cairstine is making Steenie a pony out of fabric, one he can take to bed with him, keep inside. You remember when your mama made you such things?"

Moray nodded. "I do. I loved my dog. Took the fabric one to bed with me every night. Laddies need one."

"Aye," Cairstine said. "I agree, but Steenie's sire did not. He found the fabric animal I'd made for Steenie and destroyed it before his eyes. No one will take this one away from him. Braden agrees 'tis important for him to have it."

"'Tis a great idea," Corc said.

"Aye, but I have to make one just like Paddy, so I needed to come out and study his form a bit." She circled again, and Paddy stomped his front hoof with a snort.

Her brow furrowed. "What does that mean, Corc?"

Corc shrugged his shoulders, but Celestina said, "When he stomps like that, 'tis usually to communicate a number. That meant one of something."

Paddy whinnied and pawed the dirt four more times.

"Four?" Moray asked. "Four what?"

"Four treats, usually," Corc drawled.

Paddy shook his mane rather forcefully, then pawed the ground six more times.

"Not treats," Corc said. "Then six what?"

The adults pondered the question, staring at the wee horse. He pawed the ground four more times.

"We're thinking, Paddy. No reason to be upset with us," Cairstine said, rubbing the horse's withers.

Celestina tipped her head. "Are you trying to tell us we must make four more fabric animals?"

Paddy nodded his head and nuzzled Celestina's palm, his entire body relaxing now that his message had been heard and understood.

"'Tis your answer. Paddy wishes for you to make seven fabric ponies for Steenie."

"Seven?" Cairstine asked, her eyes wide. "'Tis an awful lot for one lad."

Celestina said, "I'll assist you. Perhaps he knows of some visitors we're having. Roddy and Rose are not far from us." She shrugged. "No matter. Apparently, this is important to Steenie's dear pet, so we'll oblige him. He always seems to know what he's about."

Paddy nuzzled her hand again.

All Moray could think was that Paddy the Pony controlled more people than he did.

CHAPTER SEVEN

———◆———

JUEL STOOD NEXT TO HIS sister at the mouth of the cave, gripping her hand. "You must find us more food, Shona. The bread is nearly gone."

Jamesina stepped up on her other side. "But you must be careful. A storm is brewing. I can feel it."

"Which is even more of a reason for me to go now. If I don't find something, I may not be able to go out again for two or three days." And if it snowed, any possible food would be buried.

Juel was on his feet for the first time in days, and Jamesina's brothers had both awakened enough to sit up. They'd both suffered from sore throats, but the food had perked them up. The blessing would not last for long. They needed more food if they were truly to improve.

Shona had decided to go back to the place where she'd found the first bag of food. Perhaps the person who'd left that package, the man in the red plaid, had repeated the good deed.

Juel squeezed her hand and gazed up at her. "Promise to come back? Do not get lost."

She leaned over to give him a quick hug. "I promise to return." She knew exactly what was going on inside his head. They'd lost both of their parents. It was horrible to think that they might also lose each other.

Releasing her brother, she ushered him back toward the deepest part of the cave. "Back inside. You must stay warm,

Juel. You can play a game with Benneit and James."

"What game could we play?"

"Here," she bent over as they rounded the corner in the cave. "Use these stones. See who can throw them the farthest. Just be careful to throw them away from each other."

Shona winced. It struck her that she sounded just like her mother, but perhaps that was no great surprise. Juel was hers to protect. Hers to love.

Jamesina pulled her aside while Juel scampered off to the back of the cave. "You cannot go back to that hut. Promise me. If we lose you, we'll all die."

"I won't," she said, "but mayhap we should go back sometime. The furs alone have saved us."

"Aye, and they've been a blessing, but you were almost caught. Promise me you'll not return there? Just go quickly and return."

She nodded but wondered to herself if it would be the best blessing of all if she were not caught by that handsome Highlander.

They needed help, and soon.

The back of the cave protected them from the elements, but the temperatures were dropping. As thin as they all were, the only things keeping them alive were the heat from each other and the multiple furs they had. That and the meager food supply she'd been able to gather.

"Jamesina, I must go now before there is too much snow."

Jamesina's eyes teared up. "I know. Go before the snow is too deep but be back before dark. Please?"

"I'll return as soon as I find food for us."

She knew it was the key to keeping them all alive, and the duty of finding it rested entirely on her shoulders.

With each encounter with Paddy, Moray was becoming more convinced the animal was indeed special. Perhaps even magical. So why did the pony want him to go on patrol?

Mayhap he was going mad, but he had a niggling feeling it was over his golden-haired lass. Who was she? He had questioned Corc, Brodie, and every other guard in the keep, but no one else had seen her.

Yule would be here in another sennight, which meant Braden and Roddy should be returning soon. He called out to the guards he'd assembled for the patrol. "I want you searching not just for reivers, but for a yellow-haired lass."

Clyde chuckled and said, "I think you're having dreams of a yuletide gift that you'll not see, Chief."

Gilbert, the most serious of the three, said, "Just do as you're told, Clyde. Keep an eye out for her."

"And if I see her first?" Clyde asked with a smirk. "Bride-stealing is still allowed in Scotland."

"The hell it is," Moray growled. "She's under my protection." He pulled on the reins of his horse, moving ahead of the others. While he may not have planned to say that, he'd meant every word. They'd not touch her if he was around.

For some reason, he felt as though she *did* belong with him.

He doubted she'd agree.

His brother Ronan was the one who'd been good with lasses. He'd charmed everyone at Clan Grant. Keith had always been jealous, now that Moray thought about it. His brothers had argued quite a bit, even resorting to their fists on a few occasions. Moray had watched. As the youngest and smallest brother, he'd been able to do little else.

You might not have been able to save him even if you'd been on that cliff, a little voice whispered in his ear, taunting him. He shook it off, something he'd become accustomed to doing of late.

He rode to the reivers' camp to see if there was any sign of new activity, but he found nothing. Glancing at the place where he'd set the last sack of food, he wished he'd thought to bring another. She clearly needed it.

He even found himself taking his horse to the cottage where he'd followed her to before, but there was no sign of her there either.

Directing his horse back to the others, he held his head up to the sky. The clouds roiled in the sky, rolling in different directions, which he knew was a dangerous sign.

"Aye, Chief. 'Tis a mighty strong storm rolling in. Based on the movement in the forests, 'twill be a nasty one."

He quirked his brow at Blane, wondering what he meant.

Blane shrugged his shoulders. "Naught is moving out there. 'Tis always this way just before a wild storm hits."

And the golden-haired lass might be caught out in it. Still, with no further leads, he wasn't certain he'd ever find her again.

"Let's return," he bellowed, and the other men fell in behind him.

After a time, a whistle from the top of the curtain wall caught his attention. Someone had arrived at the castle gates. When the gate was opened for them not long afterward, his gaze immediately fell upon the visitors—a group of five men wearing an unfamiliar green plaid.

Corc said, "The MacFee is here to talk with you, Chief. 'Tis quite important."

Moray nodded, dismounting in front of the neighboring man. Although he'd heard of the MacFee, Moray was still relatively new to the area, and they had not yet met.

Moray nodded to the man, and Brodie joined them and said, "We'd be pleased to share an ale with you in my son's great hall."

"Much obliged. Who is the chief?"

"My son, Braden Grant, is laird here, but he is presently on a mission. Moray is acting chief in his absence."

MacFee greeted him briefly, his gaze assessing, but it was clear he'd prefer to speak his mind once they were inside. Moray and Brodie led the group into the great hall, and Cairstine left at once to arrange for a small repast for the group. Celestina appeared with an ale for each man at the table, Hilda assisting her.

Moray still had no idea what they wanted.

He found out quickly.

"I'm hoping you've seen my bairns somewhere," James MacFee said as soon as he sat down.

Moray glanced at him, the vision of a golden-haired lass appearing in his mind.

"A daughter and two laddies. They've been missing for a long time."

Moray's gut flip-flopped three times.

CHAPTER EIGHT

———◆———

"IS SHE GOLDEN-HAIRED, CHIEF?"

MacFee shook his head. "Nay, she and my son Benneit both have red hair, and James's hair is brown like his mother's."

Moray's hope quelled in an instant. The lass he'd seen was definitely not red-haired. "We have not seen anyone who matches your description, but if you tell us all you can, we'll be watchful. We go on patrol daily."

MacFee's face fell. "We lived in an area with five other cottages, not far from my brother, the laird of Clan Mac-Fee. My brother and I have had our differences, but I never thought 'twould cost me my loved ones."

He paused, and Moray glanced over at Brodie to see his reaction.

"You have our sympathies," Brodie said. "Tell us what happened and how we can help. We're new to this area. My son married Cairstine Muir and rid the castle of the bastards who killed her parents."

MacFee looked pleased with this information. "We've wondered why things have been calmer in this area. But I digress. Know you anything about the Channel of Dubh? The smugglers who kidnap and sell lasses and lads?"

"Aye, we do. My nieces, nephews, and son are fighting that verra group. What did they do to your loved ones?" Brodie poured the man another ale.

"The men came while we were out hunting. Killed

my wife and a few others, but they took all of the young ones. I've been searching everywhere, but there's no trail of them. It's whispered a group called the Band killed many of the men who stole my bairns, but I haven't found my sons and daughter. I've searched everywhere."

"The Band of Cousins is my son's group. They've put a stop to many bad men, including the Lamonts who controlled Muir Castle. How long ago?"

"A little over a moon ago."

Brodie sighed and leaned toward the man. "You know the odds are low they'd survive for that long in the winter."

MacFee ran his hand through his hair. "I know of what you speak, but…" He paused, his voice cracking. "But I cannot lose them all. Our three bairns, my beautiful wife… If only one of them is still alive, I must continue on."

Moray said, "You have my sympathies, but do not give up hope. I've seen a yellow-haired lass a couple of times, but she keeps disappearing. Know you who she could be?"

MacFee shook his head, his eyes misting. "My neighbor MacKinnon and his wife are dead. They had bairns, so she could be one of theirs, but I cannot say for certain. We kept to ourselves. The bastards murdered so many and stole others. Are they Scots? Who would do such a thing?"

"Who, indeed," Moray said. "We've reason to hope the Channel will be crushed soon. We've searched this area every day. Unfortunately, we've encountered more reivers than we usually would at this time of the year. We'll gladly search with you on the morrow. We'll split up the areas so we can cover more territory."

Brodie said, "You're welcome to stay the night."

MacFee stood from his seat. "Many thanks to you, but I'll not rest until I find my bairns. With the storm coming, I fear what may happen to them. Mayhap 'tis foolish, but if I can find them before Yule, I believe they will make it. But after that, the temperatures, the snow could…"

Celestina came forward with a sack and handed it to him,

putting her hand on his shoulder as a gesture of comfort. "Godspeed to you on your travels. We're happy to share cheese and bread for your journey. We wish you well."

"My thanks to you," he said. Shifting his gaze between Brodie and Moray, he said, "You'll send a messenger if you find anything?"

Moray said, "You have my word as a Highlander that we'll do all we can to find your bairns, and we'll let you know if we uncover any sign of them."

But he didn't feel good about their chances.

He would wager all three were dead or sold across the water.

———◆———

Shona crept toward the reivers' camp as quietly as she could. The air was so still that one could hear the flap of a small bird's wings as it took off in flight. While the quiet would protect her from any stranger catching her unaware, it would also alert others to her presence.

She didn't need to worry as there were no reivers in the area and, to her disappointment, no sacks of food hidden in the trees.

Returning to her favorite apple trees, she prayed to find a few new ones on the ground, but it wasn't to be. She was about to continue her search elsewhere when the sight of one apple on the ground a short distance away caught her, freezing her feet to the ground.

She'd get it for Juel.

The sound of horses' hooves carried across the glen to her, and she tipped her head, trying to gauge the distance. Not having much time to consider her choice, she shot off toward the apple and grabbed it, thrusting it into her pocket just as four horses came barreling straight toward her, the men shouting and laughing at the sight of her.

"There's one of them that ran away. She'll lead us to the others, for certes."

She spun on her heel and took off into the trees, hoping they wouldn't be able to follow on their mounts. Curses echoed through the forest behind her and she smiled, pleased to have outsmarted the bastards.

Running as fast as she could, her breath coming out in puffs of fog in front of her, she continued, knowing she was just a short distance from the cave.

Just a wee bit closer and she'd be safe.

She only broke cover when she reached the small glen she had to cross to get to the cave.

That's when they got her. A horse crashed through the brush, the rider's face dancing with glee as he reached down for her, grasping her arm and yanking it so hard it felt like it would wrench off.

"You see. I told you they were right. She'll lead us to the rest of the lads and lasses so we can get coin for them. They had to be here somewhere."

She screamed as loud as she could, hoping someone would hear her, although she prayed it would not be James-ina. Her friend was worried enough. The man tossed her across his horse face down. She struck out with her hand, her fingernails catching and clawing the man's cheek. He bellowed and punched her in the face, her head jerking back and hitting the horse's flesh.

That movement upset the beast, who did his best to buck the two of them off its back. She nearly tumbled to the ground, but a hand snaked out to keep her on the horse.

She screamed again, as loudly as she could. Two people rode up, and for a moment, her heart thrummed with hope, but apparently, they were her kidnappers' friends. They chortled and guffawed with him, enjoying her situation.

"That will be a mighty good dessert for us this night," one of the newcomers said. "We can settle soon, have a taste of her. I claim her first. She can lead us to the others on the morrow. I knew if we were patient, we'd find the ones they lost."

The man holding her on the horse said, "The hell you will. She's mine and I'll have her for the entire night before I share her with any of you."

A fright unlike she'd felt since the time she'd watched her parents killed settled inside her.

She'd stick a blade into the neck of any man who tried to touch her.

But first, she had to get away.

CHAPTER NINE

M ORAY SAID TO HIS MEN, "One more time. They could be anywhere. Search in places you've not searched before." This was their last chance for several days. The wind had steadily increased as the gray clouds made their way across the sky. The storm was nearly upon them.

The men nodded, more willing to search hard now that they knew there were young ones missing. But they'd already been searching for several hours and found nothing.

Where the hell had the golden-haired lass gone? He'd been chasing her for over a sennight at this point, and although she'd surely been a challenge, he refused to give up.

He and Gilbert were heading off in one direction when a scream ripped through the air.

A scream that came from fear and desperation. It was the lass he'd seen before. He was sure of it.

Moray tugged on the reins of his horse, sending it in the direction of the scream. When he finally managed to get close enough to set eyes upon the melee, he felt a lump in his throat. This helplessness was the same emotion he'd felt upon learning about his brother Ronan.

He'd vowed never to experience it again.

How wrong he'd been.

Six horses ahead of him tore through the trees. The reiver astride the last horse was holding a screaming lass across the saddle, face-down. Sun-colored hair whipped in the wind, telling him who he would find on the horse.

The group of horses headed across the glen, traveling way too quickly for the conditions of the ground. They raced up a ravine with steep sides—a dangerous spot where they should have slowed their pace. They did not. The last horse stumbled as they crossed the ravine at full speed. The rider fought to stay on its back, but he lost his captive.

The lass fell off the horse, then tumbled down the steep expanse, her screams ripping at Moray's insides. To his horror, he saw her head strike a rock on the way down. He shouted a command to Gilbert to continue pursuing the kidnappers, then jumped off his horse and raced down to the bottom of the ravine.

He rushed to her side, praying the blow hadn't been enough to kill her.

Her eyes were closed, and blood poured from the wound on the side of her head.

Tearing a piece of his plaid, he placed the strip of fabric against her wound, doing his best to stanch the bleeding. She moaned, but her eyes never opened.

Gingerly, he placed his hand under her chin and turned her head enough so he could get a good look at her.

Just as he'd thought, it was the golden-haired lass, only she was even more beautiful than he had guessed. He touched her shoulder and said, "Open your eyes for me, lass. Please?"

She would be covered in bruises on the morrow from her tumble down the ravine, but that did not worry him as much as her head wound. The bleeding was slowing, but the wound had swollen to quite a mound, and he hated to put pressure on it anymore.

She needed a healer.

Gilbert returned and shouted to him. "They're nearly all dead, Chief. One got away, though he's got a bad wound so he won't be back. Does she live?"

"Aye, but she will not awaken, and she has a nasty head wound. I've slowed the bleeding, but it will not stop, even in this cold temperature. We must get her to our mistresses. Settle my horse. I'll carry her up the side."

"'Tis too steep for you to carry someone," Gilbert said, dismounting and going after Moray's horse now chewing on grass.

Moray pointed to an area near the end of the ravine. "I can climb there. Bring my horse to that spot."

Placing his hands underneath her head and her knees, he lifted her carefully, doing his best not to jar her in case she had broken any bones. He noticed one wrist had swollen quite a bit, so he did his best not to touch it.

He carried her down the path before he began climbing.

"Will you make it, Chief?" Gilbert called out. "I can come down and assist you."

"Nay, she weighs no more than ten leaves on an oak tree." He didn't pass along that it was further confirmation that she was the girl who'd been taking the food. She had no fat on her anywhere.

She was starving.

When he reached the top, he handed the lass to Gilbert. "Hold her while I mount."

Once he had her settled on his lap, he took the reins and headed back toward the keep.

He sent Gilbert ahead to have Celestina ready herself for the lass, so when he arrived at the stables, Brodie, Celestina, and Cairstine were all waiting for them.

He explained what he knew and carried her inside, taking her to a chamber off the great hall. Once inside, Celestina said, "Tell me exactly what you saw, Moray."

"There's not much to tell. She was face down on a reiver's horse when the horse bucked and threw her off. They were at the top of a ravine, so she hit hard and rolled down to the bottom."

"Was she awake at all?" Celestina asked as she dipped a

linen square into a basin of water, washing the lass's face and cleaning the blood away from the wound.

"Aye, she must have been because I heard her scream, but she hit her head on a rock halfway down the incline, and I don't recall hearing a scream after that."

"Did she awaken at all on the ride back to the keep?"

"Nay. I did my best to stanch the bleeding on her head, but the lump was so big I hated to push against it. I also noticed swelling on her left wrist." He pulled her clothing back to inspect it, carefully holding it up for Celestina. "'Tis quite swollen."

Cairstine entered the chamber with fresh linen strips. Celestina said, "Moray, Cairstine will help me get her out of these dirty clothes and check her for any other wounds."

"But I'd like to speak with her," Moray said, the words coming out like an entreaty. "She could know something about the MacFees. I'll be happy to sit with her once you've cleaned her up and bandaged her where necessary."

Celestina patted his hand. "I understand. Why don't you check on your men first? Then you may sit with her later. We must wash her hair and bathe her, find her a clean gown. Seems she took quite a roll in the dirt."

"All right," he said, capitulating under duress. He did *not* want to leave her. "I'll return later."

He left the chamber, his gaze staying on the lass until the door closed behind him.

Who was she? What had happened to her?

———◆———

Moray came inside from the stables later that day but stopped as soon as he saw Brodie.

"Was Gilbert able to catch any of the reivers?" Brodie asked.

"Aye. Our guards killed all but one, and the survivor was badly wounded. The rest of our people have returned, but they haven't seen any other reivers or any red-haired lads or lasses. That storm is brewing. Promises to be something fierce."

"I wonder where Braden is. I was hoping he'd beat the storm," Brodie said, scratching his head with worry. "'Tis probably too soon to expect them. The storm should be over well before Yule, and as long as it doesn't bury us too deeply, they'll find their way back."

"Has she awakened?" Moray asked, his whole being too hopeful.

Brodie said, "Nay, her head wound is quite swollen."

"She took quite a beating rolling down the ravine." Moray would never forget the sight. It was as if he'd watched his brother take his fatal fall. If she didn't make it... Nay, he'd not think of that. "May I ask a question, my lord?" Moray used that term when he wished to demonstrate his respect for the man's position as the sire of their chieftain.

"Aye, if you'll stop calling me that," Brodie drawled.

"Should I send men out after MacFee? We promised to send a message if we located anyone who could know anything about his bairns."

Brodie rubbed his chin, considering the question. "If she doesn't awaken by morn, we could send someone out after him. See if he recognizes her."

"But on the morrow, the storm will probably be raging across the Highlands."

"Aye," Brodie said, frowning, "We'll wait until the storm subsides. We'd probably never be able to find him in the wind and blowing snow."

Moray understood this reasoning. "Do you still think Braden will make it back in time for Yule?"

"I hope so. If not, Cairstine and a wee laddie will be verra disappointed." Brodie made a motion toward the kitchens. "There's still time. I'll check on the meal since Cairstine and Celestina are busy tending to the lass. I'll see you there in about an hour."

Moray nodded, trying his best to hide his anticipation of

seeing the lass again. He made his way across the hall and knocked on the door to her sickroom. Cairstine opened it the instant his knuckles landed on the wood, startling him. "Och, Moray. I nearly felled you. I'm headed to the kitchens to make sure the meal is nearly ready. Celestina is going to check on Steenie in the stables. Would you mind keeping an eye on the lass for us?"

"Nay, not at all." He knew he should probably tell her there was no need to check with the kitchens—Brodie was already doing so—but he couldn't find it in him to say the words. She left in a hurry, and Celestina took her place in the doorway.

"She's a beautiful lass, is she not?" she said softly, giving him a knowing look. "Moray, I don't know where she was living, but she... I wish to say that I think she's been in hiding. Her clothing hasn't been washed in a while." She paused, then said, "I hope she awakens so she can give us more information."

"Do you think she knows the MacFees?" he asked, doing his best to look over her shoulder at the lass. All he saw was a glimpse of gold.

"I think 'tis a distinct possibility." She nodded to him. "Now, I must be off to see to Steenie."

Moray said, "My thanks, mistress."

He closed the door behind her, then pulled a stool up to the side of the bed. She was indeed one of the most beautiful lasses he'd ever seen. While her hair was golden, her lashes were a much deeper brown and stood out against her flawless skin. There were no freckles or anything marring her face except the bruises she'd gained from rolling down the incline.

He checked her wound, noticing someone had stitched it closed. In this one way, her unconsciousness was a blessing—she hadn't been forced to endure the pain of the stitching.

Sitting on the stool, he whispered, "Who are you? Why

did you run from me?" He brushed a stray hair back from her face. He checked everything he could, noticing Celestina had used a board to immobilize her wrist. He wondered if it was broken or just swollen and painful. She could have jammed it, which could be more painful than a break.

He reached for her hand closest to him, the one that was not swollen, and cocooned it inside both of us. "Forgive me if I frightened you, lass. My mother thinks I was driven to help you because of the guilt that riddles me over the loss of my brothers, and mayhap she speaks the truth.

"They both died this past year. Ronan and Keith. The worst of it is that Keith killed Ronan. He pushed him over a cliff over jealousy. When we learned the truth, Keith threw himself over that same cliff."

Moray stared at her closed eyes, wondering if she could hear him or not. How hard this was to admit, even to a sleeping beauty. Tears misted in his eyes when he thought of his two brothers. "I know I didn't push either of them over the edge, but it seems I could have done something. Over and over again I ask myself how I could have been ignorant of Keith's jealousy. Mayhap I could have done something to stop it. To warn Ronan."

He reached up to brush the back of his hand across her cheek. "Mayhap 'tis why I felt driven to save you. I know not. But there was…is something inside me that needed to save you. Forgive me if I took too long. Please come back."

He sat in silence for several moments, mulling over his own words. He knew he was not at fault for his brothers' deaths, but the memories stung fiercely. And he still found himself playing the what-if game. *What if I found out about Keith before he hurt Ronan? What if I was with Ronan that day?* And so on.

It was a game he played against himself.

The lass's eyes drifted open and she stared at him, pulling her hand from his. "Where am I?"

"You've been with our healer. Do not worry. We'll not hurt you."

"Is this the reiver's castle?" She tried to push herself up in bed, but she fell back onto the soft furs with a moan.

"Nay, I came after you," Moray hastened to say, horrified she might think he was the one who'd kidnapped her. "You fell off the reiver's horse and rolled down a ravine. I chased him away. I brought you back here once I was able to slow the bleeding from when you hit your head on a rock."

"My head hurts, and I'm verra sleepy." Her eyes revealed the fear and doubt inside her.

By the way her words slurred, he wondered if Celestina had given her a sleeping potion.

"Lass, what's your name? I've tried to help you before, but you always ran from me."

She closed her eyes and sighed deeply.

"Lass?" he asked. "Please. Your name. Who are you?"

"Shona." She paused and he feared she wouldn't tell him the rest. But then her eyes fluttered open again. "Who are you?" Her fingers reached up and brushed his cheek before falling down onto the bed. It felt like the caress of a butterfly.

"Moray Allen. What clan are you from? Who is your sire?"

"My sire's dead. I'm Shona MacKinnon."

One of the names MacFee had used. His heart pounded in his ears, "I have a question for you. Do you know any of the MacFee bairns?"

Her eyes flew open, making him suspicious of what she knew.

"Where am I? What castle is this?" Her words were much harsher than they'd been before. What had changed?

"This is Muir Castle. Do not worry. You are safe. Can you tell me anything about the MacFees?"

"Nay," she snapped. "I know naught about any MacFees.

But I must go. I have to return to Juel."

She was lying. He was certain.

But why?

One more thought forced its way into his mind, something he wished to ignore.

Juel.

She had to be speaking of her husband. Shona MacKinnon was already married. But he couldn't ask her about it, for her head fell back against the pillow and she was asleep in seconds.

He'd stay by her side all night, if necessary.

He couldn't let her go. Not yet.

CHAPTER TEN

SHONA WOKE UP IN A panic. She'd let herself fall asleep in Muir Castle. Given what she'd heard about the people who lived here, she was lucky to have woken up at all, though her luck was bound to run out.

She had to get away as soon as possible.

"I must go. Juel needs me."

Moray placed his hands on her shoulders. "Lass, you're in no condition to go anywhere. You took a terrible fall down a ravine, hit your head. Look at your wrist," he said. "You've been asleep for nearly two days yet you're still beat up."

That thought enflamed her panic. She'd promised Juel and Jamesina she'd be back before nightfall.

They'd surely think she was dead. She had to leave at once.

She glanced at the board and the bindings, moving it briefly enough to realize he was right about that injury. Memories of the incident itself came cascading back. That apple had pulled her, enticing her to use bad judgment. The reiver had attacked her, throwing her over the back of his horse, but the beast had bucked her off and sent her tumbling down a ravine.

No wonder her head hurt. And what was this man's part in that? Could the man who'd left food out for her really be in league with murderers?

She rubbed her wrist, just then realizing it was indeed

quite sore. Pushing herself up in bed with her other arm, she managed to sit up. "You cannot keep me here." Though her head was pounding more insistently than it had before.

"I'm sure your husband is searching for you. He'll come here eventually. You need not worry."

"My husband? I have no husband." He appeared relieved at her remark, although she couldn't think why. It didn't matter. The others were waiting for her. "I must go. You cannot keep me prisoner."

"Nay, but I must keep you from leaving now. There's a bad storm that just started. Snow and wind. You'll never be able to find your way. I'll be glad to assist you once you have proven you're capable of walking, but not until the storm is over. You'd surely die out there in your condition."

A sudden spell of dizziness overtook her, and she fell back onto the bed. Perhaps he was right. Besides, if she chose to leave at this moment, she'd regret one thing for certain.

She was ravenous. "Would you be able to get me something to eat? Some stew? Bread? Cheese? Whatever you have will do."

Moray said, "Of course."

"And something to drink. Mayhap some goat's milk?"

"Aye, we have plenty of goats. I'll be back in a few moments if you promise not to run away on me while I'm gone." He stood and moved to the door, turning around to glance at her before he left. She wished he hadn't because he had a grin that grabbed her. She'd noticed his looks from afar, but they were much more powerful up close.

Moray was a distractingly handsome man. His long dark hair fell in waves nearly to his shoulders, but it was his eyes that were most arresting. A silvery-gray color with green flecks that seemed to shimmer whenever he blinked. He had a strong chin and a small scar across one brow, but it did not detract from his good looks. She guessed he'd be a strong leader because of his unwavering gaze.

His deep voice caressed her, carrying with it the promise of a tender soul.

But how could that be if he was affiliated with Muir Castle?

"Lass?" he asked again.

She shook her head and said, "Aye, I promise not to leave while you're gone."

He left the chamber with a swagger that also caught her attention. His shoulders were as broad as the doorway and his upper arms were huge.

Ignore him! You have to get back to the cave.

She hadn't lied. Desperate as she was to get back to the others, she needed to eat to gain her strength back. Her own weakness had worsened. If there truly was a storm raging outside, she'd need a strong constitution to battle it. She probably hadn't eaten anything since she'd lain down in this bed.

She needed sustenance, which meant she'd have to wait just a wee bit longer.

When night fell, she'd sneak out, carrying as much cheese and bread as she could find. She wasn't worried about the storm since she'd traveled in the snow many times with her sire. She and Juel loved the snow—they'd even made special shoes to help them walk through it, although the shoes had been in their hut with the rest of their belongings. Everything had been destroyed.

She forced herself to sit up again, needing to gauge her ability to move about. Shifting her legs over the side of the bed, she sat on the edge, taking a deep breath before she attempted to push herself to standing.

She didn't last long before she fell back onto the soft mattress. The pain she could handle, but weakness had made her legs wobbly. Dizziness had disoriented her.

Aye, she needed to eat and eat well.

Lifting the night rail she wore, she peeked at the skin on her legs and her belly. She gasped at the darkness of the bruises, but it helped explain the aches and pains that riddled her body. A knock sounded at the door, so she dropped her gown quickly and tucked her legs back underneath the covers.

Moray stepped inside, a smile on his face. "Celestina suggested broth with a few vegetables to start. I brought some cheese that I'll leave on the table should you get hungry later when I'm not here. And here's a goblet of fresh goat's milk."

He set everything down on a small side table, then handed her the bowl of broth and a spoon. Thanking him, she set the bowl on her lap, then tasted one spoonful, moaning because of the warmth and the good taste. "You have a wonderful cook."

Moray's eyes seemed to darken as he beheld her. She felt her cheeks flush. Perhaps it had been wrong of her to be so vocally appreciative, but the soup was heavenly.

Moray looked off to the side as she continued to eat, then said, "I'll tell my mother. She's one of the cooks in the kitchens. She takes great pride in her talents."

"She should. This is wonderful. I may have to ask for another bowl." She gave him a sheepish look and handed it to him when she finished it. "Please?"

"My pleasure."

His voice came out in a husky tone, but he didn't attempt to kiss her or touch her. Instead, he nodded to her and disappeared through the doorway.

Moray Allen struck her as an honorable and trustworthy man, but her sire had told her not to trust anyone at Muir Castle. Jamesina had agreed with him.

Although her own instincts pulled at her to confide in him, she couldn't take the chance. Four people's lives depended on her making the right decision. The smart thing to do would be to take what she could and leave in the middle of the night. Hanging her head, she quickly whispered, "Forgive me, Lord. But I must take care of my brother and my friends. Find me a way out of here."

Moray had to force himself to leave the lass's chamber. He made a mental note to send someone out with a message for James MacFee as soon as the storm slowed a wee bit. After finishing the broth, she'd asked for more cheese and any fruit they had. He'd never seen a lass eat so much. The look of quiet defiance in her gaze had warned him of her stubborn streak. If he didn't keep a close watch over her, he suspected she'd sneak out. And if she snuck out, he feared he'd find her dead body deep in a snowbank in a few days.

The only reason he left was because he knew she could tell she wouldn't try tonight—she was much too exhausted to leave at present. Her efforts to stand and do things for herself were weak at best, though he gave her credit for trying.

Nay, she wasn't going anywhere this night.

He grabbed a goblet of ale in the great hall, which was almost empty. It was so late most of the clan were probably already abed. But to his surprise, the door opened and a slew of men came inside, brushing the snow off their clothing.

"We made it," Braden said, a wide grin crossing his face.

Cairstine had just reached the top of the staircase and let out a squeal as she raced down the stairs to jump into her husband's arms.

"You missed me, lass?" he said, nuzzling her neck.

"Aye," she said, distancing her body from him a bit. "You're cold."

Roddy came in behind him, his arm wrapped around his wife, Rose.

"Rose! You made it!" Cairstine wrested away from her husband and launched herself at her friend.

Braden said, "Wife, move away from the door and allow

the others in. 'Tis a freezing night out there."

"The others?" She moved out of the way, her eyes widening as more people entered.

Brodie and Celestina came down the passageway from the tower rooms where they slept, summoned, no doubt, by the noise. "The Band has returned," Brodie said with satisfaction. "A good mission, I hope."

Daniel Drummond, Braden's and Roddy's cousin, came in next, his one complete arm wrapped around his wife, Constance. He set her off to the side, then shook himself much like a dog, snow flying everywhere.

Two lads came in behind him who Moray didn't know, but then he noticed something unusual. They had each lost an arm, much like Daniel.

Celestina and Cairstine fussed over the group, taking wet mantles and hanging them on the wall while Moray moved over to the fireplace and added more wood to warm the travelers. Cairstine retrieved a tray of cheese and a loaf of bread from the kitchens, bringing it out for the group while Brodie found ales for all.

Watching the cousins, Moray had to admit he was a wee bit jealous. Joy emanated from them like light from the sun. Braden was so happy with Cairstine, and he could see Roddy was deeply in love with his wife. Although he didn't know Daniel as well, it was obvious he and his wife savored each other's company, too.

Steenie appeared at the top of the stairs, rubbing his eyes. "A party? Papa, you made it back for Yule!" He flew down the stairs and launched himself into Braden's arms.

"Aye, we've returned. Now that we're here, we'll all help you decorate, Steenie. We must make the hall festive for Yule."

Roddy said, "We'll all help."

"Hush," Steenie cried. "I made Mama and Grandmama gifts for Yule. They're 'corations for the hall. I cannot give them yet. 'Tis too early."

"Sit, sit," Brodie said, ushering the guests toward the hearth. "We have plenty of time to make the hall festive. You must warm everyone up first, get food in your bellies. We've plenty of chairs for the ladies near the fire. Moray will have it roaring in no time. The stools can be moved over there as well. Tell us all that happened. How was the traveling?"

Cairstine, her arm wrapped around Braden again, said, "I wasn't expecting you all so soon, though I couldn't be happier. Our friends are here, Steenie."

Daniel said, "We originally planned to stay the night at our castle tonight and travel on the morrow, but we pushed ahead to beat the weather. We figured we had enough guards to make the journey. Terric and Henry were eager to come with us," he said, nodding toward the two lads who were already chatting with Steenie.

A guard came inside carrying a wee lass with him. "This is Kelby," Constance said. "We've adopted the three bairns as our own. She is enamored with horses, so Owen promised to let her see all the horses before she came in."

Steenie said, "I'll show you my pony on the morrow."

"We already met Paddy. He came right out to greet Kelby," Owen said.

Steenie's grin took up his entire face as he glanced at all the people inside. "Are you all staying for Yule?"

"Aye," Braden said. "We'll have a crowd for the holiday."

Then Steenie became quite serious and said, "But what about the Dubh men? You cannot let them steal any bairns at Yule. You must fight them all."

The lad looked deeply upset—just like he always did when the Channel was mentioned. He'd nearly been sent across the waters, and he hadn't forgotten.

Braden knelt down to bring his face to Steenie's level. "You need not worry any more about the Dubh men. We put an end to them."

His gaze now wide, he asked, "You did? They're all

gone?"

"Aye, they'll not be bothering bairns any longer," Roddy said. "They'll never steal another bairn."

Daniel held his goblet of ale up. "This will be a true celebration this Yule. New wives, new families, new castles, and no more Dubh men."

Moray grabbed his ale and joined them. He was glad Braden had returned for the holiday. It certainly felt like more of a celebration with such a large, boisterous group. True, it had been a difficult, heart-wrenching year, but they had a new life. A *good* life.

He listened to the tales of the adventures the group had experienced in both Edinburgh and Berwick. They talked for a few hours before everyone split off for the night. Hilda had come inside with Corc to help Celestina make up all the chambers for the guests.

Moray and his mother shared a good-sized cottage in the inner bailey, though he often slept on one of the pallets kept in the stables. Brodie had instructed Corc to bring the pallets inside for the storm. Rather than leave the castle, Moray decided he would sleep inside in the great hall this eve. He wished to be closer to Shona, where he would be better able to protect her.

In fact, he decided to check on Shona one more time before he found his own pallet. He made his way to her chamber and knocked lightly on the door, when no one answered, he cracked it open. She slept on her side, looking like an angel if he'd ever seen one.

How he wished she was part of Clan Grant.

CHAPTER ELEVEN

———◆———

SHONA AWAKENED IN THE MIDDLE of the night—
just as she'd planned. She'd always had the ability to
wake up on command. She sat up and twisted in one
movement, swinging her legs off the side of the bed. To
her surprise, her body accommodated her.

The pounding in her head had diminished, and though
her wrist still ached along with multiple other spots on her
body, her head had cleared enough that her thinking had
improved.

Enough for her to find her way back to the cave.

Standing up, she moved over to the chest against the
wall and opened it, surprised to see it filled with clothing,
mostly tunics and trews. Apparently, whoever lived at Muir
Castle was not worried about people escaping.

Perhaps they didn't make a habit of keeping prisoners.

She fumbled through the chest until she found clothing she thought would fit, taking an extra two pairs of
woolen hose. Juel and Benneit were quite thin. They'd
need warmer socks to survive winter in the cave.

One question continued to niggle at the back of her
mind—could she trust Moray? She wanted to think he'd
bring her brother and friends back and feed them thick
stew and bread and cheese. And yet, a little voice kept
whispering to her that it might be a mistake. That he might
arrange for them to be placed in the Channel instead, and
it would be her fault for trusting the wrong man.

It didn't help that she'd overheard part of the guests' conversation in the hall. She'd surfaced to consciousness to hear them discussing the Channel of Dubh.

She couldn't make out the details, but they seemed to be cheering about the Channel's accomplishments, a sad testament to what took place at Muir Castle.

Even if Moray wasn't a bad man, and she felt certain he wasn't, one man alone couldn't help them if everyone around him was wicked. Her only choice was to gather as much clothing and food as she could and get it back to Juel and the others. She'd be out the door of the kitchens long before the castle stirred on the morrow.

It was nearly dawn before everyone had finally settled. Unfortunately, some of the guards had brought pallets in and slept in the hall, but the sound of snoring made her believe she could safely escape. After the ale they'd imbibed, she was quite sure no one would bother her.

She packed warm clothes and food into her mantle and a small sack, donned the men's trews from the chest along with her boots and clean socks, and found her way through the hall. No one budged so she crept into the kitchens, looking for any other food she could find, grabbing a meat pie to fuel her walk. When she opened the door to the back of the keep, she was shocked it was so hard to push, the wind already a force to be reckoned with. The ground sparkled with fresh snowfall, and flakes whipped through the air.

She huddled under her mantle, pulling a scarf across her face, then followed the path to a gate in the back of the curtain wall. No one stopped her from leaving. Once outside the wall, she trudged through a thick forest, grateful for the shelter the trees provided from the whipping wind.

Eating the meat pie in gulps, she followed it with mouthfuls of snow, just enough to get it down. Her breath already came in short pants, because of the cold, the snow, and the wind she battled, but she could not stop. She needed to save the others. Nothing was more important.

The wind blew snow crystals into her face, onto her eye-lashes, and even into her nose. The temperature and wind combined were enough to freeze her nose hairs, something she hated, but there was nothing she could do about it except pull her scarf tighter across her face.

She said a quick prayer of thanks to the seamstress who had sewn the wool scarf she'd borrowed because it was as tight a weave as any she'd owned, yet it allowed her to breathe through the fine openings.

The wind howled and the snowfall became heavier. She found her bearings about an hour west of the castle, slipping easily onto the many paths she'd made herself in the forest. The ground was completely covered in white, so if Moray decided to try to follow her, he'd never be able to find any tracks. A surprising sadness coursed through her at the thought. Someday she hoped to marry a sweet and gentle man, like Moray seemed to be.

But not until the evil Channel had been stopped.

The sun came up and the landscape sparkled beautifully, but the wind howled, affecting her ability to see. Would she be able to find her way back to the cave?

What if she was caught outside in the snow?

At one point, she glanced up at the sun, hoping it would help orient her, but the swirling snow whipped around her face, making it impossible to tell east from west, north from south.

Her sire had trained her on how to walk during blizzards. She knew to stay away from the hidden pockets where snow could collect in banks, and the sides of ravines where the snow could avalanche over her head, burying her. Her father had also taught her how to build a snow cave, though she prayed to make it to the cave where her brother awaited her before that was necessary. She'd always feared the thought of being buried in a bank of snow.

She took a deep breath as she approached a meadow. If

she made it across this clearing, she would reach the cave in another hour, but traversing the clearing could prove treacherous with the velocity of the winds. It would also be easy to get disoriented.

She started to cross the wide expanse, but wind spun her around and took her breath away. She trudged along sideways, but she wasn't moving fast enough.

The snow became deeper and deeper.

She could no longer see the other side of the clearing because the snow was so heavy.

Her steps faltered, becoming more and more labored.

Each boot became heavier and heavier, loaded with snow, packed with extra weight. Each knee had to be lifted higher and higher to clear the sheer depth of snow.

You must keep going. Think of Juel, Jamesina, Benneit, James. You must…

You must…

If she closed her eyes just for a moment, she could take a short nap on this soft snowbank she'd fallen into.

Just a quick nap…

———◆———

Moray had gathered a group of men to help him search for Shona. Still stunned that she'd had the fortitude to gather food, dress as a lad, and leave the keep, he had to give her credit and assume she'd made it a distance away.

Yet this blizzard would not be easy to travel in.

Paddy the Pony bucked against his stall as if eager to join them. The three lads, Terric, Henry, and Steenie, did their best to calm him. They'd run out to the stables with the guards despite the adults' best efforts to keep them back inside the castle.

"He's afraid of the storm. We must let him out," Steenie begged.

But Braden wouldn't be swayed. "It's plenty warm enough for a pony inside the stable. He's too short to wander around in a blizzard. One deep snowdrift could bury him alive."

Corc said, "I'll stay behind with you lads. Henry brought a few apples for the pony. Paddy will be fine once the others leave."

Eager to leave, Moray set out with Roddy, Braden, Daniel and a couple of guards. They fanned out crossing the terrain, looking for any tracks, but the snow was falling too quickly. They didn't dare separate because they'd easily lose their bearings and each other. They continued on, looking for any sign of a lass.

The more time that passed, the more worried Moray became. They huddled together inside a group of trees at one point. Braden said, "I see no sign of anyone out in this weather. She didn't steal a horse, so she has to be on foot. How could she have gotten away that quickly?"

Moray said, "She's quick on her feet. 'Tis all I know. We have to find her. She'll die alone out here."

"Mayhap she returned home," Braden suggested. "She must have been living somewhere. Or she found a stray reiver's horse from the attack the other day. 'Tis definitely a possibility."

"Where? We know all of the cottages in the immediate area," Moray insisted. "I fear she's alone."

"I agree with Moray," Roddy said. "She's living alone somewhere, but there's only so much we can do."

Braden said, "We'll search for one more hour, then I'm ordering everyone back to the keep. I'll not be losing any of you over a lass who could be safely ensconced in her own place somewhere. No one asked her to leave—she did so of her own free will."

Much as Moray felt the desire to search all day and night, he had to agree with his chief. His own fingers were getting mighty cold. They all knew the serious repercussions of spending too much time outside in the snow.

An hour later, Braden whistled and led them back to the

keep.

Moray feared she was buried in the snow, possibly even dead. He hated giving up. Hated it. And yet, he didn't wish to risk anyone else's life. They moved the horses into the stables, warming themselves at the same time. The building was incredibly well built, a structure that barely whistled with the wind. Cairstine's sire had done a fine job of building this castle for his clan.

Corc had cups of warm broth for those who'd been out in the cold, and the hot liquid quickly warmed up Moray.

Paddy was still having a fit at the end of the passageway. Moray made his way down, still holding the bowl of broth in his hands for the heat. "Steenie, has he been this way the whole time?"

Steenie said, "Nay, he just started again when you returned."

"Come, I'll help you find him some carrots to calm him. Where are your friends?"

"Terric and Henry went inside to warm up. We were all inside for a while, but when I saw Papa had returned, I came back out."

They collected the treats from the bin at the front of the barn, walking around the other men who were still savoring their broth, then turned around to head back to Paddy's stall.

Only he was missing.

"Hellfire, but I latched that stall," Moray whispered to himself. "Stubborn beast."

Steenie cried, "Paddy, where are you?"

He got more and more upset as they searched the stables for him, but he was nowhere to be seen. How had the wee beast crept past all of them? The others were still gathered near the entrance. Surely they'd have seen him.

"He left," Steenie cried out. "We have to go after him. Please?" He ran to Braden and stared up at him, clearly hoping his adoptive sire would take up the search for his dear pet.

Braden set down his broth and shot to his feet. "Corc, come with us for a moment."

The group of four stepped outside just in time to see Paddy leaving through the gates, tossing his mane and letting out a snort over his shoulder.

Moray said, pointing to the departing figure, "The wee beast is laughing at us."

Braden said, "Send Roddy out with three horses, Corc. We'll go after him. Steenie, you're to wait inside the great hall with Corc."

The three mounted quickly and headed out the gates, surprised to see Paddy not far ahead of them. He'd taken off in the same direction they'd gone earlier, to search for Shona, although he'd paused. Almost as if he were waiting for them to follow.

Moray glanced at Braden and said, "Do you think the animal knows something we don't?"

Braden shrugged his shoulders and said, "'Tis Yule. Believe as you wish, but never doubt him, my sire says. We have to follow him."

"Aye, animals are known to do strange things," Roddy agreed.

Moray yanked on the reins of his horse, praying Paddy would take them to Shona.

CHAPTER TWELVE

———◆———

THEY FOLLOWED PADDY FOR QUITE a distance, far longer than they would have guessed, although it didn't surprise Moray that Shona would have gotten this far. The lass was persistent. Strong.

Moray glanced over at Braden and Roddy each time the wee beast took an unexpected turn, but they all followed him without question.

Paddy seemed to know exactly where to walk—he never sunk too far beneath the snow, although Moray's horse dipped down until half his forelegs were covered.

Finally, they moved across a meadow, snowdrifts and wind howling as if nature were unleashing her fury on someone. Paddy stopped abruptly, buried his muzzle into a deep snow drift, then lifted his head and whinnied.

Moray stopped his horse and dismounted, running to the spot where Paddy's snout had been. Sure enough, there was the tip of a wool scarf.

Moray dug at the snow like a man possessed, praying at the same time. When he uncovered her head and pulled the scarf away, he waved to Braden and Roddy, who jumped down to join him.

"Is she still alive?" Roddy asked, searching for her feet.

"I think so," Moray said, removing his glove and putting his hand in front of her face. "I feel warmth and a small breath, I think."

"Hellfire, 'twould be a miracle if she survived this."

Roddy scanned the area as the brutal blizzard continued to pound on them. "Who knows how long she's been in that drift? It could be minutes or longer."

Braden bent over and dug as fast as he could. "I told you before," he said, panting, "'tis Yule and 'tis Paddy. Miracles happen. We've seen them before with the animal. He brought us here, did he not?"

"Lift her out," Roddy said. "We cannot wait to get her back to the keep. We'll have to take her to a protected area and warm her."

"How the hell are we going to warm her?" Braden asked.

"There's only one way. One of us will have to undress her and give her our heat. She'll never make it back like this."

"I'll do it," Moray said at once.

Braden said, "She's uncovered. Where can we take her? Do you see a protected area?" Their gazes searched the area, but then Paddy snorted and headed off in a new direction.

Braden's eyes widened. "I'll not question him." Turning to Moray, he said, "Get on your horse and I'll hand her to you. Follow the possessed pony."

Moray did as Braden suggested and followed the wee horse. Sure enough, Paddy led them to a cave.

Roddy whistled as they stepped inside the small covering. "Hellfire, he *is* possessed. A spirit lives inside him. It must be. 'Tis a perfect place. I'd have never found this spot because it's so well hidden. You strip her down and we'll start a fire."

Moray sat down on the cold stone and settled her on his lap.

"Shona, 'tis me, Moray," he said. "I'll not hurt you." He unbuttoned her mantle, tossing the wet garment off to the side, then looked to Roddy for direction. "And the tunic also?"

"Aye, we'll dry it by the fire so you can put it back on her for the trip home. Leave her chemise on. Your heat will carry through it. But you must get her warmed up first or she'll not make it back. The color on her face is not good. 'Tis the first thing my mama checks."

Braden said, "I'll see if I can find any dry wood for the fire."

Paddy joined them inside the cave, still making strange noises. He moved to the back then emerged with a mouthful of sticks, dropping them at Braden's feet.

"What the hell, Paddy? Is there something else you wish to tell us?"

The wee horse snorted, but Braden and Roddy focused on getting a fire started.

Moray removed his mantle and his plaid, then pulled off his tunic, leaving his trews on. He took a deep breath and pressed her cold body up against his own, gasping as her frigid skin touched his flesh.

"Best part of men, Mama always said. We're forever warm," Roddy said with a smile. "Here, I'll wrap your plaid over her back to keep her from losing your heat."

He knew it was working because he could actually see the color of her skin changing. Her lips, which had been a dusky gray, had already taken on a light pink tinge. The blush moved across her skin as if someone were waving a wizard's wand across them. It wasn't long before her eyes opened.

"Moray?"

"Aye, we found you in a snowbank. You had a wee angel watching over you. 'Twas foolish of you to leave in a storm."

"My brother…"

Braden stopped what he was doing and rushed over. "What did she say?"

"She said something about her brother."

Paddy bucked and snorted again, then moved into the back of the cave. Shona lifted her hand and pointed in that direction.

Moray picked her up, wrapping the plaid around her, and followed Braden and Roddy back into the cave.

"Saints above join us, please," Roddy mumbled.

There in the back of the cave were three lads and a lass. The only one alert was the lass. She had a strange sobbing sound coming from her, but she shed no tears. "Shona. Is she dead?"

Moray said, "Nay, she lives. Who are you?"

"Help us, please. We'll not live much longer. We have no food."

Braden bent down and picked up the smallest lad, while Roddy moved to the others.

"Are you from the Channel?" the lass whispered. "Are you going to steal us away?" The odd sobbing sound continued to come from her.

"Nay," Braden said softly. "The men from the Channel are no more. We're from Clan Grant, and we live at the Muir Castle. What's your name?"

"Jamesina. These are my brothers, James and Benneit, and the smallest lad is Shona's brother, Juel."

"Why are you hiding in this cave?" Roddy asked.

"We're hiding from the Dubh men who killed my mother and tried to steal us all away. They killed Shona and Juel's parents. Please help us. We're hungry and cold..." She hugged one of the wee lads to her chest. "Benneit, wake up. Someone is here to help us."

Moray asked, "Is James MacFee your sire?"

"Aye," Jamesina replied, hope in her gaze.

"Fear not. He's looking for you, and he'll return to Muir Castle. I've already sent a messenger for him."

"Juel?" Shona whispered.

Juel opened his eyes and Braden brought him over so Shona could see him.

The lad asked, "Shona, are you hale?"

"Aye."

Jamesina stood up, helping her brother stand. "Where

did you find Shona? She never returned to us. I feared she was dead."

"The reivers caught her when she was searching for food. She rolled down a ravine and hit her head. We brought her to our castle to our healer, but then she crept out when we were sleeping. We found her in a snowbank, then we came here to warm her so she could awaken."

She gave him a strange look and asked, "How did you know to look here?"

Paddy shook his mane and turned back toward the entrance, snorting over his shoulder as he took his leave.

Braden whispered, "Paddy magic."

CHAPTER THIRTEEN

———————

MORAY AND HIS FRIENDS HAD saved them, and the Dubh men were no more. It truly felt like a Yuletide miracle. When they stepped back into the keep with Shona wrapped up in Moray's plaid, a big burly man shot up from a trestle table. "Jamesina! Benneit and James?" He rushed over to them, a look of shock on his face.

Moray led Shona to a chair by the hearth, and Juel sat on her lap and rested his head on her shoulder as they watched the tearful reunion.

It was the first time Shona had ever seen a man the size of James MacFee shed tears. He cried and cried, hugging each of his children individually before setting them down on the trestle table around him. It felt bittersweet to watch them. Although she was happy for her friends, she knew she and Juel would never see their parents again.

As if he sensed what she was thinking, Moray reached down and squeezed her hand.

"I cannot thank you enough, Moray," MacFee said at last.

Moray said, "You owe thanks to Braden, our chieftain, and the wee horse who led us to Shona and the cave. We'll do that later. He's celebrating with three carrots and an apple at present."

MacFee ushered his three children over to the hearth. Someone had brought out a huge tray of meat pies, and Shona and Jamesina and the boys all helped themselves. James MacFee sat in a chair and stared at them, as though he feared they might disappear if he took his gaze from them. The man choked up as he watched them eat, their hunger evident. "You're all so thin."

James moved over to his sire and leaned against his knee. "Don't cry, Papa. We'll be fine. Shona and Jamesina kept us alive and 'tis the most important. 'Twas because of them that we got away."

MacFee hugged his son and nodded, again and again. "You are right. I'm grateful. We'll always miss your mama, but we will survive. I've found you and 'tis what I'll focus on." He wiped his eyes and glanced at the chieftain, Braden, who'd just come inside to sit by the hearth. "You and your people saved my children's lives. If you have room, I'd be honored to join you here at Muir Castle. When we returned, your stable master told me you're welcoming hard workers. I was a smithy for my brother, and I'd be honored if you'd allow me and my bairns to live here with you. I have two men with me who'd gladly join your guards if you're in need, Chief. The other two will be returning to Clan MacFee."

"You don't wish to return to your brother's clan?" The question had been asked by an older man who looked a lot like Braden. His father, perhaps. He came forward and joined them.

"My brother and I have mended our differences, but he already has a talented smithy. I'd be pleased to join a clan where my talents can be of use. If you need time to think about it, please do. I would ask that we be allowed to stay until the Yule or at least until my bairns are hale enough to travel."

Braden smiled at MacFee. "We'd be honored to have you join us here. There are not many of us, so you'll have to work hard, but we could use a man with your talents, and we could certainly use more guards. Your lads are nearly old enough to start training in the lists."

"Aye, in another couple of years. They can assist me or

work the soil. Jamesina has a fine hand with a needle. Her mother, bless her soul, taught her well."

A pulse of loneliness passed through Shona. Where would they go? They had no home to return to, but they also had no special skills to offer. She gave Juel a squeeze, but he leapt off of her lap and scampered over to stand in front of the three big Highlanders—MacFee, Braden, and the man who looked like Braden. "What about us? The Dubh men killed both of our parents. We have nowhere to go. May we stay?"

Braden and the man who looked like his sire said in unison, "Of course."

"We'd love for you to join us," Braden added. "We have plenty of room and extra foodstuffs for winter."

Just then, the door burst open and a wee lad ran over to the hearth. "More lads? Are they staying, Papa?"

Braden said, "Benneit and James will be staying with us, Steenie. Juel here just asked if he and his sister could stay. What say you?"

"Aye! I'll have friends! Juel, you can sleep in my chamber with me if you like."

Juel looked to his sister before he answered. "May I, Shona?"

The lovely, calm lady who'd helped Shona earlier came in, followed by Braden's wife, Cairstine, the surviving Muir. "We'll find a chamber for the lassies to share so Juel can join Steenie," Cairstine said at once. "We'd be pleased to welcome you all." She moved over to Shona and lifted her out of her seat, wrapping her into a warm embrace. "You poor things. My sympathies for all you've had to bear, but you are all verra strong if you've survived the Highland weather at this time of year."

She glanced over at Moray, still standing behind her, and he nodded, a pleased expression on his face. "We have a fine clan, and we—*I* would be honored if you'd join it."

Steenie suddenly jumped up and down.

Cairstine entered the hall and asked, "Steenie, what is it?"

"Paddy. He's the smartest of all. You'll see soon!

Shona had no idea what the lad was about, but life was suddenly improving.

They had a home again.

———————◆———————

The keep had been a flurry of activity ever since the Mac-Fees and Shona had joined them. Celestina and Cairstine had set themselves to the task of arranging bedchambers, pleased that they had enough for all. They stayed inside for another day until the storm finished lashing its fury on them, then they gathered in the great hall to decide where everyone would fit best.

Not wanting to take one of the few remaining chambers in the chieftain's keep, James MacFee had insisted that his family would do quite well in one of the two remaining cottages inside the bailey. Roddy, Rose, Daniel, Constance, and Shona had all gone outside to assist them with the cleaning of the cottage.

Midway through the day, Moray knocked on the door and asked to speak to Shona. She came to the door, a bright smile on her face. It was the kind of smile that made it impossible not to smile in return.

"You've healed quickly, lass."

"Better than Juel, but I think he will do quite well in another day. He's quite happy playing with Steenie and Paddy, so I left him in the stables."

Moray shifted from one foot to the other, not sure how his request would be received. "Shona, the blizzard has ended. Would you mind going for a stroll with me so we could talk?"

She glanced back at Jamesina, Rose, and Constance, who were all nodding their heads furiously, grins on their faces.

"Aye, allow me to grab my mantle."

Once they left the cottage, Moray took her hand, leading

her outside the gates so they could speak privately.

"'Twas a nasty storm, but 'tis quite beautiful now, is it not?" she asked as they strolled through areas where the wind had cleared the snow for them.

"Aye, nature can be as beautiful in the winter as it is in the warmer months." He cleared his throat, nervous about how to best approach her.

She stopped and tugged on Moray's hand. "Moray, I must thank you again for your dedication in searching for me. Had you not been willing to follow Paddy through the blizzard, I'm sure we'd have all died in the storm."

"Please, you've thanked me many times and you need not thank me again. 'Twas my honor to assist you." He cleared his throat and fumbled through different ways to approach her. It struck him that perhaps he would do best to be direct, so he said, "'Struth is, I'm interested in you. I would like to court you. Would that be acceptable to you?"

She smiled and tipped her head. "You're a fine man, Moray Allen."

Moray's heart skipped a beat. Was she suggesting they might suit? "Those are verra kind words, Shona. Does that mean you would consider…"

She leaned forward and tugged his face down to hers. "Kiss me."

He groaned and touched his lips to hers, tentatively at first, but then he angled his mouth until she parted her lips, allowing him to taste her sweetness. Hell, he'd never been as happy as he was at this moment. His desire for her built to a feverish pitch, but he kept it carefully under control. When he ended the kiss, he cupped her face in his hands and kissed the cold tip of her nose.

"I couldn't let you go," he said softly. "There was a part of me that believed we could be together, if only I could find out why you hid from me. I'm not verra experienced, and I don't know how to go about this in the right way, but I'm most pleased that you'll consider my suit."

Her brow quirked, and he cursed himself. What the hell had he been thinking to be so forward? Then tears flooded her face and he didn't know what to do.

"Forgive me. I'm sorry. Forget what I said. I didn't mean to make you cry." He'd surely made a mess of things. He should have kept his mouth shut and kept his feelings to himself.

"'Tis not that. I'm happy, and aye, I'd be pleased if we could get to know each other better."

His heart skipped a beat. He must have heard her wrong. "You would? But we just met. My heart is sure of what it wants, but are you certain you feel the same?"

She chuckled, a sound he hoped to hear again and again. "Moray, I wanted to trust you from the first, even when I worried you might work for the men who hurt the Muirs. I think Mama and Papa guided you to me," she said, tears misting her eyes. She hung her head as the tears fell onto the snow beneath her.

"If you keep that up, they may freeze on your face," he said, hoping to lighten her mood. Loss was something he understood all too well.

She smiled, swiping the tears away. "Having you by my side will make the holiday easier for me, although I miss my parents terribly." She paused, then added, "I'm verra glad you felt the need to help me. If you didn't, I don't know what would have happened to us. But your brothers... I was so sorry to hear of your troubles, but 'tis not your fault."

"You remember what I said?" he asked, shocked.

"Not right away, but I did last eve. 'Tis another reason I know you're right for me. You have a good heart."

He kissed her again, then said, "I'd like to introduce you to my mama if you don't mind."

"I would love to meet her."

He took her hand and led her back into the inner bailey. "She's busy cooking in the kitchens. The morrow is Yule, and they've planned a big feast to celebrate. All the guards will be inside, everyone in the clan. I'd be pleased if you'll share a table with me."

"Aye, and Juel. Will your mother be able to join us?"

"After she meets you, I'm certain she'll make a point of it."

They passed the MacFee cottage on their way to the keep and the sound of applause reached their ears. They spun around at the same moment.

"Well done, Moray," Braden yelled out.

Roddy said, "Another wedding coming soon, if I were to wager."

Moray grabbed a fistful of snow, quickly forming it into a snowball, and hefted it at Braden, hitting him in the shoulder only because he turned.

Moray then wrapped his arm around Shona and hurried her toward the door, protecting her from the barrage of snowballs hitting his back, laughter echoing across the bailey.

CHAPTER FOURTEEN

THE KEEP AT MUIR CASTLE was full of revelry the eve before Yule. Steenie, in particular, seemed overjoyed to be approaching the holiday with his new friends. He'd taken Juel under his wing at once, for which Shona would be eternally grateful. She watched with a smile as Steenie bustled about the hall, leading her brother around as he toted two small sacks.

"The morrow is Yule, Juel. This eve we'll have a great big feast. We have pheasant and Papa even caught a boar. He and Grandpapa got it fresh this morn. We'll have boar stew and pheasant soup. And Hilda makes the best fruit pies. You'll see. And Papa brought some spices back from his travels near the sea."

He made his way over to the women decorating the hall. "Mama? Grandmama? I have something for you." He leaned over to whisper something to Juel, but she couldn't hear his words. Whatever it was made Juel giggle. The two were perfect together.

"What is it?" his mother asked, turning to face him. His grandmother spun around also.

"Here. Happy Yule to you both!" He handed each of them a sack, his face beaming with pride. "I worked verra hard on them."

Cairstine peeked in her sack and gasped. "Oh, Steenie. This is quite beautiful. You must have had help with this." She pulled out a basket full of greenery, red berries, ribbons, and pine cones.

"I did it almost all by myself. Be careful. There's a place to put water inside so the branches won't die."

Celestina's basket looked similar, although the ribbons had been arranged differently. "Oh, Steenie. This is magnificent. I love it!"

Steenie giggled when they each came over to give him a hug. His mother said, "I'm putting mine on the dais."

His grandmother said, "I'm placing mine on the hearth mantle for now, but I must take it to my chamber at night so I can enjoy it all day."

Steenie whispered to Juel, "'Tis so much fun giving presents. You'll see! Next year we'll do it together."

They'd all helped with the decorations inside the great hall. Celestina, Cairstine, Rose, and Constance had woven garlands of plaids and evergreens. One particular table held a huge basket filled with pine boughs and ribbons.

"But what is this table for?" Steenie asked, running up to the empty trestle table, still hand in hand with Juel. "Why did you put it here in the middle of the hall, Grandmama?"

"Why, this is for your gifts, Steenie," Celestina said. "Do you not recall all the ones you made?"

"Aye, I do. But what shall I do with them?"

"You'll hand them out at the meal this eve," she said, rushing to the kitchens. "We'll let you know."

Shona joined them and whispered to her brother, "Juel, do not expect gifts. They did not have time to make anything for us."

"I have to go," Steenie announced, tearing out of the keep.

Juel asked, "Where did he go?"

Shona said, "He'll return, I'm sure." Juel wasn't able to keep up with Steenie yet, but she was sure he'd be chasing behind him in another day or two.

"I think he went to get his gifts and bring them inside," Juel said softly.

An hour later, the feast began, and everyone assisted in bringing the food out, while Hilda and Moray's mother instructed everyone on how they wished to have the food arranged. The meal was delicious. Shona sat with Moray and his mother at the dais with Braden and Cairstine, Steenie and Juel sat together across from Brodie and Celestina. Roddy, Rose, Terric, Henry, Kelby, Daniel and Constance sat at the long table near them with the MacFees.

The other tables were full, as the guards had joined them for the feast. It was a loud and joyous meal together, laughter bouncing off the rafters.

When they finished eating, Celestina whispered to Steenie, "Why don't you get your gifts now, Steenie. You can hand them out."

Steenie raced over to the table, picked up his packages wrapped in twine and hurried from person to person, handing out the carefully wrapped packages.

Shona was more surprised than Juel when Steenie handed him a long package. But nothing surprised her more than when she had a package dropped on the table in front of her, one much smaller than Juel's but a package, nonetheless.

"Go ahead. Everyone open your gifts," Steenie cried as he moved back to stand between his mother and father. The sound of fabric unfolding filled the hall, and Steenie couldn't contain his giggles. "Grandmama, this is so much fun. You're right. I like giving gifts."

Shona watched Juel open his and his eyes widened, his jaw dropping open when he saw the finely hewn wooden sword inside. It was just his size. He picked it up and ran his hand down the wood. "Someone took a long time whittling that, Juel. Make sure you thank Steenie. He must have worked verra hard on it."

Juel stared up at her. "Open your package, Shona. I wish to see yours."

She glanced at Moray, who nodded with a smile. "Go

ahead."

Her hands shook when she opened it, and she glanced at Moray, who said, "'Tis not from me. 'Tis from Steenie. I have a small gift for you, but open this one first."

She unfolded the fabric carefully, gasping when she saw the beautiful ribbons inside, perfect for her hair. The sight nearly brought tears to her eyes.

"Shona, just like Mama always had for you," Juel said.

"Aye. I must go thank Steenie." She got up from her chair, tears misting her eyes at her good fortune. Moray and his clan were a true Yule miracle.

Juel raced over to see Steenie already surrounded by all the other lads—Terric, Henry, James, and Benneit. They each held a sword just like he did.

Jamesina held a handful of ribbons exactly the same as Shona's. Her gaze caught Shona's, her look of delight evident from across the hall.

"Steenie, many thanks to you. How did you know 'twas exactly what I needed? And the lads all love the swords."

"Paddy. He told me I had to make five swords so I did. Then he said I had to put ribbons in packages, but he never told me why. He is magical. I tell everyone he talks to me, but they don't believe me. See…he knew you were all coming."

She'd heard the tale of Paddy the Pony, of course, but she still marveled over the fact that the wee pony had led Moray to her. She reached for Steenie's hand and asked, "How does he tell you things, Steenie? He cannot speak."

"I hear it in my mind. Then I know. He never explains why, he just tells me things."

Shona peeked up at Moray and asked, "Is he really that special? How did you know to find me? To find us?"

Moray shrugged his shoulders. "He led us to your location in the middle of the storm. Besides leading us directly to you, he also led us to the cave, and he knew exactly where to go in the snow. He never got caught up in a snowdrift at all."

Everyone had quieted in the hall, listening to the tale of Paddy and his gift.

"'Twas naught but a miracle lass, a Yuletide miracle," Braden said. The others agreed.

"There are more," Cairstine said. She motioned to Celestina to assist her in handing out the rest of the packages.

There were carefully wrapped packages for each family. Celestina had made some of her oils for the lasses, Cairstine had made chair cushions for her friends' new castle. Dried meat was also shared to be taken home.

While they were busy opening their packages, Moray pulled one from the table and brought it to her. "For you, Shona."

Shona's eyes lit up at the carefully wrapped package. "I have no idea what it is," she whispered to him. She opened it carefully and inside was a scarf in the Grant colors, red, green, and black. "Moray, 'tis most beautiful." She ran her fingers over the finely woven wool. "My thanks, but I did not have the chance to find a gift for you."

He leaned over and whispered in her ear. "You're all the gift I need."

She blushed and stared at her gift. "I'd never guessed things would turn out this way."

Cairstine caught everyone's attention with her last statement. "And these last gifts are the most special. Special because Paddy again gave us some insight into how many were needed. Many hands went into crafting these gifts." She beckoned to Celestina and the two handed out the gifts, one for each child under the age of ten. Each was given a fabric animal. Henry and Terric's faces lit up when they saw their fabric dogs. Henry said, "I've always wanted an animal to go to bed with me."

Wee Kelby squealed when she opened her fabric bunny, complete with a fluffy white tail.

Steenie opened his gift and squealed. "Paddy! I have

a wee horse to take to bed with me. My thanks to you, Grandmama and Mama. I love Yuletide."

Just then, there was a loud pounding at the door.

Braden glanced at his sire, who shrugged his shoulders, but then moved over to answer it.

He opened the door and groaned.

Paddy, who'd kicked the door with his hind legs, turned around and pranced into the hall to the applause of everyone present. Once he reached the middle of the great hall, he turned around and flicked his tail to one group and his mane at the other. Both tail and mane had been wrapped and plaited with ribbon.

"All right, back outside, you wee beast," Braden said.

"Just a moment, Braden," Moray said. "Allow him to stay a moment more, if you don't mind."

Braden nodded, although he gave him a surprised look. Moray headed over to a chair, bending over to grab something he'd hidden behind it.

A small basket filled with apples and carrots.

"What is that for?" Braden asked.

Brodie said, "Not what, but whom?"

"I'll answer both at once," Moray replied, carrying the basket over to Paddy the Pony. "'Tis for all he's done for us."

Braden chuckled as the small horse turned about in a circle, almost as if he were gloating.

Moray set the basket down in front of the pony.

"A little thank you for all your Paddy magic," he said. "I'll never doubt you again, you wee trickster."

Paddy turned his head to Braden and showed all his teeth.

Just as if he were smiling.

Brodie lifted his goblet and said, "Happy Yule to all."

~THE END~

DEAR READERS,

Wherever you are, whatever you celebrate, a verra happy Yuletide to all!

Keira Montclair

www.keiramontclair.com
www.facebook.com/KeiraMontclair

NOVELS BY KEIRA MONTCLAIR

THE HIGHLAND CLAN
LOKI-Book One
TORRIAN-Book Two
LILY-Book Three
JAKE-Book Four
ASHLYN-Book Five
MOLLY-Book Six
JAMIE AND GRACIE- Book Seven
SORCHA-Book Eight
KYLA-Book Nine
BETHIA-Book Ten
LOKI'S CHRISTMAS STORY-Book Eleven

THE SOULMATE CHRONICLES
#1-TRUSTING A HIGHLANDER

THE SUMMERHILL SERIES- CONTEMPO-RARY ROMANCE
#1-ONE SUMMERHILL DAY
#2-A FRESH START FOR TWO
#3-THREE REASONS TO LOVE

STAND-ALONE NOVEL
FALLING FOR THE CHIEFTAIN-Book Three in
Enchanted Falls Trilogy

ABOUT THE AUTHOR

KEIRA MONTCLAIR IS THE PEN name of an author who lives in Florida with her husband. She loves to write fast-paced, emotional romance, especially with children as secondary characters in her stories.

She has worked as a registered nurse in pediatrics and recovery room nursing. Teaching is another of her loves, and she has taught both high school mathematics and practical nursing.

Now she loves to spend her time writing, but there isn't enough time to write everything she wants! Her Highlander Clan Grant series, comprising of eight standalone novels, is a reader favorite. Her third series, The Highland Clan, set twenty years after the Clan Grant series, focuses on the Grant/Ramsay descendants. She also has a contemporary series set in The Finger Lakes of Western New York.

Her latest series, The Band of Cousins, stems from The Highland Clan but is a stand-alone series.

Contact her through her website:
www.keiramontclair.com

Made in the USA
Coppell, TX
05 April 2020

18431183R00056